**"You have thirty seconds. Then I walk out,"** Ares warned in a soft, dangerous murmur.

Odessa believed him. After all, hadn't he done that once, this man who was a world removed from the younger version she'd known? Or was he?

Hadn't he possessed this overwhelming presence even back then, only caged it better?

Now the full force of it bore down on her. Odessa was at once wary of and drawn to it, like a hapless moth dancing toward a destroying flame.

She watched, mesmerized despite herself, as his folded arms slowly dropped, his large, masculine hands drawing attention to his lean hips, the dangerously evocative image he made simply by... *being*.

At what felt like the last second, she took a deep breath and took the boldest leap. "Before my father's memorial is over, Vincenzo Bartorelli will announce our engagement." Acid flooded her mouth at the very thought. "I would rather jump naked into Mount Etna than marry him. So, I'd...I'd like you to say that I'm marrying you instead. And in return..." *Dio*, was she really doing this? "And in return, I'll give you whatever you want."

## A Diamond in the Rough

*Self-made billionaires claim their brides!*

To commemorate Harlequin's 75th Anniversary, we invite you to meet the world's most irresistible self-made billionaires!

These powerful men have fought tooth and nail for every success and know better than most how hard life can be. They've overcome significant obstacles, but will they be able to overcome the greatest obstacle of all...love?

Find out what happens in

*The Italian's Pregnant Enemy* by Maisey Yates

*Hidden Heir with His Housekeeper* by Heidi Rice

*The Tycoon's Diamond Demand* by Joss Wood

*Signed, Sealed, Married* by Annie West

*Greek Pregnancy Clause* by Maya Blake

And watch this space—there are more seductive Diamond in the Rough heroes coming your way soon!

# GREEK PREGNANCY CLAUSE

## MAYA BLAKE

**Harlequin**

## PRESENTS

**Harlequin®
PRESENTS™**

ISBN-13: 978-1-335-93906-7

Greek Pregnancy Clause

Copyright © 2024 by Maya Blake

Recycling programs for this product may not exist in your area.

For questions and comments about the quality of this book, please contact us at CustomerService@Harlequin.com.

TM and ® are trademarks of Harlequin Enterprises ULC.

 Harlequin Enterprises ULC
22 Adelaide St. West, 41st Floor
Toronto, Ontario M5H 4E3, Canada
www.Harlequin.com

**Printed in Lithuania**

MIX
Paper | Supporting responsible forestry
FSC® C021394

**Maya Blake**'s hopes of becoming a writer were born when she picked up her first romance at thirteen. Little did she know, her dream would come true! Does she still pinch herself every now and then to make sure it's not a dream? Yes, she does! Feel free to pinch her, too, via Twitter, Facebook or Goodreads! Happy reading!

## Books by Maya Blake

### Harlequin Presents

*Reclaimed for His Royal Bed*
*The Greek's Forgotten Marriage*
*Pregnant and Stolen by the Tycoon*
*Snowbound with the Irresistible Sicilian*

### Ghana's Most Eligible Billionaires

*Bound by Her Rival's Baby*
*A Vow to Claim His Hidden Son*

### Brothers of the Desert

*Their Desert Night of Scandal*
*His Pregnant Desert Queen*

### Diamonds of the Rich and Famous

*Accidentally Wearing the Argentinian's Ring*

Visit the Author Profile page
at Harlequin.com for more titles.

# CHAPTER ONE

IT WAS A spectacularly beautiful day to become an orphan.

Despite the profoundly sacrilegious thought, Odessa Santella breathed in deep, letting the salt-tinged sea breeze fill her lungs, tilting her head to the sunrays in the hope it would reach her cold, frozen insides. She dug her bare toes into the rough pebbles beneath her feet, willing the discomfort to ground her.

Opening eyes she'd squeezed shut, the better to experience this monumental day, she watched dappling light bouncing off the water, ignoring the craggy cliff face, the sheer drop and the jagged, deadly rocks ten feet beyond where she stood.

It was indeed a beautiful day to—

A rough throat was cleared behind her, shattering her peace—such as it was.

'Signorina.'

The prompt held warning, as most of her interactions with anyone connected to her father had for as long as she could remember.

It didn't matter that her father was dead. That she was minutes away from witnessing the final rituals following his death. She would never be free of him. He'd seen to that in the meticulous, cruel way he'd ruled her life.

Odessa took one resigned step back, then another, her pitch-black dress growing heavier on her body as the breeze dropped away and the weight of fate pressed down on her. Taking another moment, she slid her black pumps back onto her feet.

She'd thought she'd be free once Elio Santella had succumbed to his cancer.

*How foolish she'd been!*

A hundred yards away, two dozen pairs of eyes watched her approach, each set evaluating her, wondering whether she would become a problem they'd have to deal with or whether she would, like all the other women in the family, *know her place. Stay in her place.*

One set in particular made her skin crawl. Dark as soot. Deadly as a viper.

Vincenzo Bartorelli had revealed his intentions the second Odessa had turned twenty-one. It had only been through a series of mishaps keeping him out of her father's good grace that she'd been saved from his unwanted advances for the last seven years.

Now, with her father out of the picture, this man who was over twice her age all but salivated every time he clapped eyes on her. And he'd made sure those occasions were frequent since Elio's death a week ago.

Hell, he would've all but moved into the twenty-bedroom mansion her father had called his castle but Odessa termed her prison, if Uncle Flávio hadn't called first dibs on the property he'd not so secretly coveted since his brother had built it thirty years ago.

Her gaze slid over to her uncle, hoping for some sign that the nightmare hurtling towards her was all in her fevered imagination. The harsh look reprimanding her for keeping everyone waiting and warning her not to make a scene eviscerated any such hope.

His eyes trained on her, he tapped his hand against his leg in silent summons—a demeaning cue he'd picked up from her father. She wanted to yell that she wasn't a dog to be called to heel. Pursing her lips, she slowed her feet and lifted her chin, her heart thumping as his eyes narrowed.

No doubt her rebellion would earn her punishment before sundown, but she'd grown accustomed to verbal lashes and the occasional backhander.

At some point she'd decided that not behaving herself was worth it.

It kept her soul from shrivelling and dying.

She slotted herself into the too-narrow gap between her two living tormenters and stared down at the casket containing her dead one.

Her father had grown more bitter and vicious in the months before his death. The news that his illness was terminal had warped him into a crueller version of the previously tyrannical mob boss everyone feared. Faced with his dwindling mortality, Elio hadn't sought to go peacefully. He'd railed against fate and everyone who came within ten feet of him, blaming everyone and everything but the expensive cigars he'd inhaled every day for five decades.

Odessa listened to the priest intone words of peace and salvation. Her lips twisted. Her heart was unable to wish this man who'd tormented her for so long rest. She hoped her mother gave him hell in the afterlife, the way she hadn't dared when she was alive. She hoped—

Her thoughts stalled, then scattered as the muttering around the graveside rose.

*'What are they doing here?'*

*'Is that really him?'*

*'I never thought I'd see him here ever again.'*

*'Have you heard how powerful he is now?'*

That last statement jerked Uncle Flávio's attention away from the priest, power and influence being the twin drugs he rabidly fed on. When he wasn't boasting about how he'd acquired them, he was greedily plotting nefarious ways to gain more.

Odessa, knowing she would inevitably be trapped in whatever web his plans created, redirected her attention from her father's casket too, her heart squeezing in dread at whatever calamity was approaching. Because she'd learned to her cost that there was always, without fail, a worst-case scenario with the Santella family.

Following the gazes of the mourners, realising even the priest's words had trailed off, she blinked away tears she didn't remember shedding.

Then her heart stopped altogether.

What *was* he doing here?

Because this was truly the last place she'd expected to see him.

Aristotle Zanelis.

*Ares.*

The name exploded in her head like the earth-shaking feats of his Greek namesake.

In the years since she'd last seen him he'd conquered the world, moulded it to his will and made himself a formidable force to boot.

He wielded the kind of power Flávio and Vincenzo would give their limbs for. And he was here, at her father's funeral?

Belatedly she saw the smaller man striding at his side.

Sergios Zanelis—his father. The man who'd chauffeured her father for the better part of twenty years until crippling arthritis—and her father's unscrupulous behaviour—had forced the gentle Greek to retire.

'Who invited *him*?' Flávio barked, but already she could hear the thirsty speculation in his voice, the fervid scramble to work this angle to his advantage. She felt more than saw his hard eyes drill into her temple. 'Did you—'

'No,' she interjected strongly, still unable to take her eyes off the towering, broad-shouldered man who bore down on them as if he owned the very land he walked on.

Odessa would've speculated that he probably did—considering his international real estate mogul status these days—if she hadn't known for a fact that the mansion she'd been born in now belonged to her uncle.

Besides, considering how they'd parted ten years ago, she wouldn't have dared to reach out to Ares for anything—never mind condolences for her father, who'd treated him as deplorably as Elio had.

*What about what you did?*

Vines of shame and righteous indignation twisted around her heart, strangling her as he drew closer. Or was it the sheer magnificence of the man who'd lived up to every promise of the drop-dead gorgeousness his younger self had predicted?

Because...*angeli sopra*...Ares Zanelis was carved from the very best of celestial moulds.

'Who is this?' Vincenzo snapped.

Flávio stepped away without answering, crossing the grass towards their unexpected guests. Completely ignoring the senior Zanelis, her uncle held out his hand to Ares, his initial vexation totally eradicated by his covetous smile.

Odessa's heart leapt with alarm when Ares's hand remained at his side, his face formidably imperial. But she watched his lips move and a tense second later Flávio was transferring his greeting to Ares's father, who shook his hand and nodded solemnly.

Only after the older man had been greeted did Ares shake Flávio's hand. The whole spectacle lasted less than twenty seconds, but it was shockingly clear who'd gained the upper hand in the little exchange.

Odessa gasped as her wrist was trapped in a crushing grip.

'Answer me when I talk to you, girl,' Vincenzo growled beside her, sensing the balance of power shifting and petulantly resenting it.

'Let go of me.'

Her demand was low and hoarse. His cruel grip and the knowledge that later she would be sporting a bruise hollowed her stomach in an unmistakable portent of what was to come.

She tried to snatch her hand away, but he merely tightened his hold. About to protest further, she froze when Ares Zanelis arrived next to her, his imposing body blocking out the sun.

'Release her.'

The rough and viciously animalistic growled command raised the hairs on her nape. As did the gaze he concentrated upon the man holding her captive. Its savagery caused Vincenzo's eyes to widen in swift alarm as he quickly heeded the order.

His will imposed, Ares redirected his gaze to her.

Odessa rubbed her stinging wrist, tilted her head up and up—had he always been this tall?—and met the cold liquid hazel gaze of the man who had dominated her thoughts once upon a time. But while she'd been able to read his expression back then, he was now a dark, impenetrable tower, content simply to stare at her without uttering a word.

In her teens, she'd likened his heart-stopping demeanour to one of the mythical Greek creatures of old. Even back then his dominance had been unquestionable.

That aura was a hundred-fold more potent now, and the ferocity of it snatched the air out of her lungs and accelerated her heartbeat.

Her alarm that he was here, in the place he'd left without so much as a goodbye, mingled with her nerves as she cleared her throat. 'I... Ares... Thank you for coming.'

Odessa was painfully aware that her statement lacked warmth and held a definite query.

'It isn't me you should be thanking,' he replied, in a voice that had definitely deepened with time, and once again warning tingles danced over her neck and shivered down her spine.

Before she could ask what he meant, his father was stepping up to her, the older Zanelis' trademark smile dimmed only by the solemnity of the occasion.

'Odessa, it is good to see you,' Sergios Zanelis said, reaching out to grasp her hands in a much gentler hold. 'I hope you don't mind that we're here, but I insisted we pay our respects. Your father was generous enough to keep me in his employ for over twenty years. I will never forget that.'

Ares's jaw clenched at his father's words, and an absurd hollow opened inside her. It couldn't have been clearer that this was the last place he'd have come if his father hadn't insisted on it. Or that his father's positive outlook didn't match Ares's own view of past events.

Telling herself that she might easily have gone another few decades without clapping eyes on Ares Zanelis would've been a lie. For one thing, he dominated the news these days, his power and influence a source of breathless material for both mainstream and social media.

That was how she knew he was unmarried. How she knew his relationships barely lasted a handful of months, with the princesses, actresses and supermodels of this world who apparently lined up round the block for a chance to be his latest flame getting the revolving door treatment with eye-watering frequency.

That was how she knew his father was the only constant in his life.

When she'd read about the car crash that had almost taken both their lives four years ago it had sent her to the tiny San-

tella family chapel every sunrise for the three weeks Ares
had remained in a coma in California. And in that chapel
she'd made fervent promises she hadn't been sure she'd be
able to keep.

Aware of the thick silence, and especially of Ares's laser
gaze boring into her, Odessa cleared her throat and summoned a whisper of a smile. 'It's very good of you to come,
Mr Zanelis. I really appreciate it.'

And she did, because in this sea of men with nefarious
intentions and a willingness to mow everyone down including her—*especially* her—in their bid to become the next
head of the Santella organised crime family, seeing this man
who'd gone about his work with an incredibly sunny dispo-
sition was a balm she couldn't help but greedily latch on to.

She grew even more conscious of Ares's stare as she
spoke, his scrutiny sharpening over her face as if gauging
the veracity of her words.

The priest clearing his throat pointedly gave her the excuse to turn away. To face her father's casket once more.
She kept her gaze fixed on it even while her senses whirled
in frantic alarm as Ares took Vincenzo's place at her left
side, with his father displacing Uncle Flávio on her right.

And it was in the thirty minutes as the service resumed—
as her uncle's dark eyes moved speculatively over her and
Vincenzo's gaze promised hell—that the seed of her desperate idea was born.

Because, while she'd been unable to read Flávio's expression fully, she'd seen it enough before—deciphered that
look after she'd spotted it countless times on her father's
face, and on those of most members of her family and his
so-called business partners.

Resentment. Judgement. The promise of retribution.

In Ares's eyes she'd spotted something else. The ghost
of an emotion she'd thought long dead.

*Lust.*

Awareness of the feeling she'd thought had been left behind when he'd walked away from her that fateful night drew from her fresh tingles of danger and partly shame. But, while this occasion was the last place she should be thinking of such things, his proximity, his aura... Dear God, even the way he smelled—like thunder-tossed rainstorms and smoked wood—was undeniable and erotic in its invasiveness.

And if she wasn't wrong about what she'd seen in his eyes maybe she could...

*God, could she?*

She drew in a shaky breath as the priest ended the ceremony. As she tossed the white rose she'd plucked from the offered vase onto her father's lowered casket and mourned the parent not for his death, but for what he'd never been able to give her in his life, she knew, deep in her bones, that she needed something to change.

Remaining under Flávio and Vincenzo's already strangling hold would be the end of her. But, just as she knew that, she also knew that merely running wouldn't work.

Her move needed to be bold. Drastic. Terminal in a way that burned bridges neither Flávio nor Vincenzo could repair. Because if she didn't...if she was somehow half-hearted in this...

A tremor shook through her and Ares's sharp gaze swung to her.

Pushing the frightening thought aside, she glanced around her and noticed the mourners were slowly dispersing, while casting furtive glances at the two men stationed on either side of her.

Feeling another presence behind her, Odessa glanced over her shoulder. Flávio stood there, but his beady gaze was fixed squarely on Ares.

'Zanelis, there's a reception back at the house. We would

be obliged if you would attend,' he offered, disingenuous charm oozing from him.

Again, Ares's face tightened at this deliberate snub of his father, even though the older man seemed unconcerned.

After an age of his gaze never leaving hers, he answered tightly, 'If that is what Odessa wants.'

The sound of her name on his lips, with that slight evocative Greek accent which had remained despite his spending most of his formative years in Italy, made her pelvis tighten.

Regardless of his words, though, his eyes told her to refuse. That it wasn't what *he* wanted. Righteous indignation rose again. He had a nerve to hold a grudge. What she'd done back then had been to protect him. While he…

He was her last hope, no matter how bleak and spurious her idea might turn out to be. No matter how aloof and hostile he seemed now, she would cling to the memory of the less intimidating man she'd known back then. The man who'd whispered promises to her beneath the stars…

Because she couldn't let Ares leave. Not yet.

'I would like that very much.' She ignored her uncle's smug expression and turned to Sergios. 'If you have the time, Sergios?'

She was playing a risky game, exploiting the past affection the older Zanelis had had for her. She prayed she would be forgiven her transgression. Ares's narrowed eyes when she glanced at him from the corner of her eye said he'd seen through her ploy. Still, she kept her eyes fixed squarely on his father.

'Of course, my dear,' Sergios responded, immediately offering his arm.

Relieved, she clung to him all the way up the hill, back to the house that had been a prison for as long as she could remember.

Nearing it, she examined the imposing facade closely.

Had the vines creeping around the windows always been this dense, almost suffocating the structure as the house did her? Had the drapes framing the thick bulletproof windows always been this gloomy? Every door, stone and blade of grass was in pristine shape, of course. The staff were trained to fear, and knew that flaws wouldn't be tolerated under any circumstances and that they would sometimes be severely punished for infractions.

Case in point, the sweet man walking beside her, who'd been summarily sacked the moment his arthritic fingers had become an imperfection her father hadn't been able to tolerate.

Odessa had moped for months after Sergios had left the Santella household, even as a part of her had been soothed by the thought that he was reuniting with Ares.

Ares, the man whose contempt pulsed from him as he strode in tense silence beside her.

*Ares, the man she intended to use to grasp her freedom.*

Thoughts of the perilous road ahead made her shudder, and her step faltered momentarily before Sergios's surprisingly strong grip held her up.

'The loss may seem insurmountable right now, but it will lessen,' he said, mistaking her stumble for grief. 'It will never go away, but you'll learn to live with it.'

She felt like a fraud, accepting comfort when she didn't miss her tyrannical father one little bit. When she knew that once she escaped—*if* she escaped—she would never set foot on this cursed soil ever again.

Far too soon they were inside the largest *salone*, the place where Elio had held court and lorded his superiority over his subordinates.

It was in this very room that he'd told Sergios his services were no longer required because he was old and useless.

It was in this very room that he'd told her never to speak to Ares Zanelis again, *or else*...

It was here, only a few short months ago, that he'd told her he would be marrying her off to Vincenzo Bartorelli, a man older than he himself, to consolidate his power.

Odessa avoided this room unless strictly necessary. The dark green furniture was stiff and uncomfortable, the thick residue of cigar smoke hanging in the air too cloying. It was a room where men made plans about women and expected them to bend or break to accommodate them.

No, she would not miss this room one little bit.

She thanked one of the maids offering her a tray of drinks and chose a mineral water, needing to keep every wit about her. She rarely drank anyway, and when she did it was at functions where refusing would draw her father's disapproving glances.

In fact, the last time she'd been anywhere near tipsy it had been with...

Her gaze flicked to Ares as she wondered if he remembered that night on her seventeenth birthday, when they'd sneaked out at midnight and sat on the cliff-edge with a stolen bottle of her father's Dom Perignon. How they'd lain on the grass, the backs of their hands touching under the canopy of stars with the raging waters beneath their feet. How they'd whispered their hopes and dreams to one another.

Did he think of her at all? Had he spent a single moment on *what if*?

'Does it hurt?'

She started, then followed his gaze to her reddened wrist, where imprints of Vincenzo's cruel hold were already proclaiming her fate if she didn't find a way out of this nightmare.

'Um...not really.'

His face darkened, hazel eyes turning molten bronze. 'Either it does or it doesn't. Which is it?' he grated, not bothering to keep his voice down.

'Okay, it's a little sore,' she muttered, hyper-aware that they were the centre of very speculative attention—especially from Vincenzo Bartorelli.

She tensed when, after a moment of dark observation, the older man started across the room, his destination unmistakable.

Panic rising, she turned to Ares. 'Can I talk to you?'

One jet-black eyebrow lifted. 'What makes you think we have anything worth saying to each other? I'm only here because of—'

'Your father. I know. But…' She swallowed, wondering if she shouldn't find another way between the rock barrelling towards her and this man who'd disappeared from her life once already. But the sands of time were fast slipping through her fingers. Ares might be a devil, but at this point he was the lesser of two evils.

'Please,' she whispered. 'It's important.'

A mix of curiosity, censure and suspicion darted across his face. Her heart squeezed, threatening to mourn, because there'd once been a time when only curiosity and amused interest dashed with the intoxicating and forbidden had existed there.

'Important to you, perhaps. Not to me.'

His gaze flickered past her to where his father was speaking to the butler, another man who'd been in the Santella household since long before Odessa was born.

'I don't intend to be here long enough for whatever—'

'Odessa. A moment of your time?' Vincenzo interrupted, a hard edge in his tone.

Her heart plummeted. She knew what was about to happen. She'd heard whispers of it, and seen enough of Flávio and Vincenzo's clandestine meetings in the past week to know.

She darted an imploring gaze at Ares, uncaring if he read the naked plea in her eyes. He didn't say a word…not for a long stretch of time that shredded every nerve in her body.

Then, when she thought she'd have no choice but to seal her fate by publicly refusing Vincenzo, Ares bit out tightly, 'It'll have to wait. Odessa's wrist is sore. It needs immediate attention. So if you'll excuse us…'

It wasn't a request for permission. It was a pointed barb that struck true from the look on Vincenzo's reddened face as his gaze dropped to where he'd gripped her so mercilessly.

He opened his mouth, no doubt either to excuse himself or to belittle Ares's comment. Either way, he wasn't given the chance.

'Shall we?'

At her nod, Ares's firm fingers wrapped around her elbow and he led her towards the closest door.

Relief lightened her feet—until reality set in. She had the opening she sought, but she was nowhere near home free. There was still a mountain to climb.

But as she walked beside the man she'd once thought would be hers for ever, she knew there was no going back. There was no way she would marry Vincenzo Bartorelli.

If she didn't succeed, she'd simply have to find another way. She would rather die than live beneath another man's thumb.

With uncanny accuracy, considering he hadn't stepped foot inside this house for over a decade, and even back then he'd rarely been permitted indoors, Ares led her down two long corridors, bypassing her father's study to enter the small library.

Unlike most rooms in the Santella mansion it was nondescript, almost bordering on simplistically pleasant. It had been her mother's favourite room only because her father had hated it and spent the least money on it in his grand villa plans.

Odessa had dreaded her father turning it into another gaudy showpiece after her mother had died, but for whatever reason Elio Santella had left it intact. It had become Odessa's favourite room in the house…the place she felt closest to her mother.

Was that why Ares had brought her here? Did he remember?

The way he turned his back on the bookshelves and view, facing her with narrowed eyes and arms folded, said that he probably didn't.

'Thank you for your time.' She paused, cleared her throat. Would he agree to her outrageous proposal? 'I…'

'Spit it out, Odessa. I don't have all day.'

Irritation bit into her, sending her chin up before she could stop herself. 'I need your help,' she blurted.

For the longest time he eyed her, his focus unblinking. 'Let's bypass your assumption that you have the right to ask anything of me and skip to the part where you believe I would *want* to help you in any way.'

Her heart juddered at his acid tone. The last remaining ounce of her pride screamed at her to walk away, hold her head high and fight the fate barrelling down on her another way.

But the way he'd dealt with Vincenzo just now shoved aside her pride and bolstered her hope. 'Look, I wouldn't ask if I didn't need… Besides, you…' *Owe me*, she'd been about to say. But she bit her tongue against revisiting that part of her past, and what she'd done to ensure his safety.

'I what?' he demanded, eyebrows raised and with no ounce of give in his features.

She shook her head, dismissing the unsavoury consequences she'd had to bear for simply associating with her father's chauffeur's son. 'It doesn't matter.'

She couldn't think about the past now. Not when her future was so bleak—

'You have thirty seconds. Then I walk out,' he warned in a soft, dangerous murmur.

She believed him. After all, hadn't he done that once before, this man who was a world removed from the younger
version she'd known.

Or was he…?

Hadn't he possessed this overwhelming presence even
back then, only caged it better?

Now the full force of it was bearing down on her, Odessa
was at once wary of and drawn to it—like a hapless moth
dancing towards a destroying flame.

She watched, mesmerised despite herself, as his folded
arms slowly dropped. His large, masculine hands drew attention to his lean hips, the dangerously evocative image
he made simply by…*being*.

Silence ticked away, and she watched that eyebrow slowly
arch, as if he was surprised by her audacity in letting her
chance whittle away.

*Go big or go home.*

Except this home was one she was desperate to escape.

At what felt like the last second, Odessa took a deep
breath and took the boldest leap. 'Before my father's funeral
is over Vincenzo Bartorelli will announce our engagement.'
Acid flooded her mouth at the very thought. 'I would rather
dive naked into Mount Etna than marry him. So I'd…I'd like
you to say that I'm marrying you instead. And in return…'

*Dio*, was she really doing this?

'And in return I'll give you whatever you want.'

# CHAPTER TWO

It was only because he kept such a rigid control over his emotions that Ares didn't burst out laughing. Even then, an abstract part of him barked raucous laughter in his head, while another part grew intensely furious. Not with her. Or perhaps a little with her... Because, *Thee mou*, hadn't she dragged confounding emotions out of him from the very first time he'd laid eyes on her?

*'I'd rather dive naked into Mount Etna...'*

That snatched glimpse of melodrama was one of many reminders he'd tried to forget about her. That it had triggered a different sort of amusement made him stiffen.

He wasn't here to traipse down memory lane. Or be reminded of everything he'd hoped for during those foolish years of his youth.

He'd once dreamed he'd be the one offering a life-changing proposal. All these years later, and with the benefit of hindsight, he knew he'd had a lucky escape. Yet his chest continued to tighten as he looked at her now, this insanely beautiful woman who had only grown maddeningly more alluring in the years since he'd last seen her.

He should dismiss this nonsense, march back into that room he hadn't been permitted to enter as the son of the boss's chauffeur, insist to his father that they were leaving.

That this was indeed the absurd idea he'd suspected it was when Sergios had suggested it.

The look in her eyes—appeal battling with the pride she so very staunchly hung on to—stayed him. Was that all that was stopping him leaving? Or was it that taunting, delectable little addendum she'd thrown in?

*'In return, I will give you whatever you want.'*

He hated himself further for the memory those words evoked…for the time when he'd craved just that from her.

*To have her. To walk away. Never look back.*

Wouldn't that make him as bad as the very people he despised with every fibre of his being? Men like her father? Her uncle? That cretin Bartorelli, with his too-harsh thuggish hands and slimy lust in his eyes?

'I know you heard me,' she muttered, then pursed her lips, drawing his attention to her mouth.

The full mouth that he'd only had the opportunity to taste once before it had been wrenched away from him. The mouth she'd used to betray him, casting him aside as if he was nothing.

'Say something,' she pushed at his prolonged silence.

'Are you sure?'

Her beautiful eyes blinked. 'What do you mean, am I sure?'

'Do you really want me to say something? Because there's a high probability that you won't get the answer you wish if I do.'

She swallowed, and again his gaze was compelled to that part of her body, noticing how smooth her neck was, how creamy and so very inviting.

He clenched his gut, unwilling to be led by desire down another disastrous road littered with betrayal.

Her chin lifted another notch, and perhaps that was the catalyst that stopped him from walking away. Because the urge to master that pride and defiance, watch her crumble completely, slowly shattered his resolve. The need to win, just for once, in this insane situation with Odessa Santella trumped any other need.

That she would dare to flaunt her pride in the face of apparent abject hopelessness was a challenge he couldn't resist.

'Yes, I want to know your answer,' she replied, her voice firm, her eyes boldly locked on his. Daring him to tell her no.

Again, he felt that urge to laugh—an absurdity in this situation that should never even have occurred. But then didn't his father continue to stump him with his own unique outlook on life? And hadn't he vowed a long time ago never to be like his father?

As much as he loved him—and he did, with an unfettered well of affection that had surmounted their many challenges—he still couldn't accept or forgive how his father had allowed himself to be treated by the Santellas. What his misguided devotion had cost his own family before he'd been chewed up, then spat out, disposed of with barely the clothes on his back when he'd outlived his usefulness. Yes, the ultimate betrayal lay with his mother, but Ares couldn't help the sliver of bitterness for what his father's own actions had prompted.

'Very well then,' he said, taking perverse pleasure in the statement. 'My answer is…no.'

Pride and defiance deflated like a pricked balloon, her shoulders sagging. She went pale, her bottom lip trembling for a second before she firmed it. Her most unique trademark, the Santella silver eyes that had haunted his dreams for far longer than he wanted to admit, darted around the room, then returned to his face, searching, as if unsure whether to believe him or not. He held her gaze, infused his own with ruthless purpose until her eyes dimmed in acceptance.

'I see.'

Silence reigned, and he found himself holding his breath, gut clenched tight. In anticipation of what? He realised that he was waiting for something more from her. For her to fight harder for him?

*Yes.*

When he registered that she wasn't going to speak, a disarming confusion bubbled inside him, which triggered more volatile emotions.

She wasn't going to fight now, just as she hadn't fought back then. Was it because, despite seeing him as a last resort, she still deemed him inferior? Or, he amended cynically, was it because she'd chosen to make herself clear back then in a very different way by betraying him with another?

'If you don't wish to marry that idiot with his too-eager hands, why don't you simply tell him that?'

Sparks lit her silver eyes, her mouth twisting. 'Surely you haven't forgotten how things work around here?' she threw at him.

His mouth soured. No, he hadn't forgotten. But wasn't she the princess of the castle? Or, better yet, the queen now? 'Your father's gone. Surely you're free to do as you wish now?'

Bitterness pinched her mouth, drawing his eyes back again to the sensual curve of it, the soft, velvety plumpness that made heat flow with eager abandon through his pelvis. It was an unwelcome indication that in some ways things hadn't changed. This woman still drew effortless sensations from him.

'You would think so, but apparently he's made sure he rules my life even from the grave.'

His jaw clenched. The recollection of the ruthless, power-hungry brute Elio had been—a man who put his interests ahead of everything and everyone, including his own daughter—was a bile-inducing one. Ares had batted off the threats and taunts from the crime boss, but the betrayal from Odessa still dredged up fury and bitterness that lingered.

It especially chafed that he hadn't managed to make the old man pay for the way he'd treated his father. He'd thought he had time—had been stunned when his father had informed him that Elio had succumbed to cancer mere months before his sixtieth birthday.

Coming here today, it had crossed his mind briefly to make the daughter pay for her father's transgressions, but he'd discarded the idea.

Odessa had enough of her own sins to account for.

*'Anything you want...'*

The idea tantalised him far too much. Made his shaft thicken as he fantasised ways to enact his own sweet brand of retribution.

Footsteps echoed outside the door.

Odessa's gaze darted to it and he watched her face grow haunted.

Rage mounted—both at the thought of Bartorelli being responsible for that look, and at the fact that he utterly loathed the thought of that man touching her.

Hell, the idea of *any* man touching her drew an uncustomary red glaze across his eyes. He told himself that it was because he despised bullies, and every male member of her family deserved that label. But when it came down to it Ares suspected it was that tempting little addendum that made him reach out to stop her jerky step towards the door, one arm wrapping around her waist and the other cupping her chin to redirect her focus to him.

And just like when he'd led her out of the *salone*, that sensation of her skin beneath his fingers made his breath catch.

He accepted in that moment that he'd forgotten a few things about Odessa. Dear God, she was as soft and yet firm as he remembered. And that little sound she made in her throat as she faced him was equally intoxicating, twice as dangerous.

"'I see"?' he echoed sardonically. 'That's all you're going to say?'

The sparks flared in her eyes, turning them molten and mercurial, in shades he'd found far too fascinating back when he'd known no better.

'You want me to beg?' she goaded. 'Is that what you're waiting for?'

*Oh, yes.*

'That would be a good start.'

Her nostrils quivered—a delicate sight that sent yet another shock of heat through him.

'I didn't imagine you'd become a sadist.'

'Looks like we're learning new things about each other.'

*And obsessing far too much about old things. Like what would've happened if you hadn't betrayed me.*

She opened her mouth, perhaps to berate him. He never found out, because in that moment, knuckles rapped hard on the door.

She flinched. His teeth gritted. *Ne*, he hated that reaction in her. Just as he hated everything about this day.

Then his mood darkened even further, as the door started to open without his express permission.

Acting solely on instinct, he dropped his hand from her chin. Then, wrapping his fingers over her nape, he tilted her face up to his.

'We will discuss this further in a while. But for now...'

Sealing his mouth on hers, Ares gave in to the deep, dark temptation that had stalked him ever since he had spotted her at her father's graveside.

He swallowed her soft grunt of surprise and swept his

tongue through her parted lips, tasting her with a hunger he partly despised and partly welcomed, because perhaps he might need this further down the line, when he exacted due retribution.

He hadn't altogether decided which way he was going to go, but *this* was a good start.

Dragging her closer to his ravenous body, he gloried in the soft curves that seemed sculpted to his, that flashed reminders he didn't want, but couldn't resist.

She gave a throaty moan and opened her lips, her hands coming up to wrap around his waist. He couldn't help the rumble of satisfaction that erupted from his chest. So many things he'd been denied with this woman were finally achieving reparation.

He didn't need to assure himself that he could have had her any other way, but it helped that she was as helpless to this strain of insanity as he was.

In the years he'd been gone from this place he'd had a glut of liaisons—enough to satisfy him that he didn't need any one person…especially a forbidden princess named Odessa Santella.

Yet here he was, devouring her as if she was the sole reason he drew breath.

Ares ignored the pointed throat-clearing from across the room and tangled her tongue with his, unable to resist one last taste.

It came again—louder, insistent.

Odessa pulled back sharply, her hands pushing at him as she tried to put distance between them.

Deliberately or reluctantly—he couldn't be sure—he took his time in releasing her, lifting his head to lock his eyes on their unwanted intruder.

'Flávio.'

If Ares had despised Elio, his younger brother came a

close second simply because he'd been more than happy to ride his brother's thuggish coattails and carry out his orders without compunction. Flávio had been the messenger who had gleefully delivered Elio's poisoned edict, which had triggered the events that had sent Ares away from this place.

He watched the other man take in their embrace, watched his calculating eyes working out how to turn it to his advantage. Ares's mouth soured, but still he didn't release her.

'I don't remember giving you permission to enter.'

Flávio's eyes blazed momentarily with malice. Ares knew that ten years ago Flávio would've reacted differently. And, yes, he knew there was definite satisfaction in watching the other man mind his tongue. Just as he knew that by challenging him he'd made Odessa's situation ten times worse.

So did she, by the way she stiffened and then tried to push away from him.

'Stay.' He rasped the warning in her ear.

For a microsecond she heeded him, and then the innate rebel smothered by years of oppression fought back, tossing another log onto the fire blazing within him. Her body brushed his, bringing an unwanted reminder that he was fully aroused at being this close to her, and he felt her soft breath against his jaw, smelled her spicy scent in his nostrils.

He hissed as her movement brought her wrist over his engorged flesh. Ignoring Flávio, Ares slid his finger beneath her chin, bypassing her swollen lips to snag her gaze.

'If you want my help you'll do as I say.'

She stilled after another second, her eyes narrowing on his. He wanted to remind her that he never said anything he didn't mean. But what use was that reassurance when he knew the same didn't apply to her? She'd heeded his command when it mattered. That was a good start. Her rebellion would be enjoyable in the right setting.

Registering that he was making plans as if this was a forgone conclusion disconcerted him, but he hadn't achieved success beyond his wildest dreams by not being able to think on his feet.

'You're still here, Flávio. Can we help you?'

Odessa made a tiny, protesting noise, her eyes flashing wildly at him. He slid a soothing hand down her back before he could help himself.

'My niece's presence has been missed. It's her father's funeral, after all. We don't want to raise questions.'

Ares laughed. 'You don't? Because you care about impropriety?'

Flávio's gaze dropped to his hand on her waist and his face tightened. 'Odessa is a good woman. It won't do to have her honour questioned.'

'We both know her honour isn't why you're here. Run along. We'll be out shortly.'

'You shouldn't have done that,' she murmured once Flávio had departed, the hard click of the door signalling his displeasure.

His gaze dropped to her mouth, savage hunger tearing through him. 'Which part? The part where I reacquainted myself with how surprisingly sublime you taste? Or getting rid of your uncle?'

Colour surged into her face and he itched to trace it with his fingers. Then his mouth.

'Both! You may enjoy baiting a viper, but I don't.'

He drifted his fingers down her arms, delighted in the shivers that raced after his touch. 'Hmm…let's go and find out how effective we've been, shall we?'

Catching her fingers in his, he tugged her after him.

'Ares, what are you doing?' she hissed.

Something hard and hot and decadent punched through him at hearing his name on her lips after all this time. The sexy Italian huskiness of her voice had first turned him on as a callow youth—the chauffeur's son enchanted by the princess in the dark castle. It partially grated that its erotic effect hadn't entirely waned.

Perhaps it was a good thing, he mused. A heightened libido wasn't altogether bad.

He continued until he'd reached the door of the *soggiorno* and then, pausing in full view of the guests, he cupped her delicate jaw. 'Anything I want. Those are still your terms, correct?'

Her silver eyes grew saucer-wide, her pupils dilating as her tongue emerged to dart nervously over her bottom lip. 'Ares—'

'Yes or no?' he pressed. A rabid need was pounding through him, filling his ears with an unstoppable roar.

She sucked in a breath, the awareness that she was caught between a rock and one immovable Greek visible in her mercury eyes. The longest three seconds of his life dragged past. Then…

'Yes,' she answered, and that punch of bold almost-dare kicked like a narcotic in his blood. As if inviting him to do his worst.

*Just wait,* s'agapo. *You'll see.*

Triumph equal to or perhaps even surpassing what he'd felt after his last multi-billion-dollar real estate deal surged through him. But he wouldn't celebrate just yet. He knew better where this woman was concerned.

'You'd better hope that your oaths mean more to you now than they did all those years ago, *agapita*. Because trust me when I say you'll regret it otherwise.'

Warning delivered, he dropped one hand but left the other in the small of her back, using it to draw her close as they faced the now hushed room.

Slowly he took in people's expressions, cataloguing which

men would pose a problem and need handling, noting the ones eager to get into his good graces. His gaze lingered longest on Bartorelli, saw the moment the other man recognised he'd been bested.

Then Ares's gaze shifted to his father.

Up until that moment he hadn't been entirely sure he'd go through with this madness...whether he would only go far enough to ensure Odessa was removed from the threats that dogged her—for a yet to be determined price but no more. Because she was and should remain where she belonged.

*In his past.*

But the flash of hope that arrived and then lingered on his father's face as it darted between him and Odessa sealed his decision.

Ares kept his gaze on Sergios for another second, then glanced down at the woman who'd held a compulsive fascination for him once upon a time. Who, he admitted, continued to have an absurd grip on him that he needed to rid himself of once and for all.

Ne, *perhaps she'd handed him the very tools to do so...*

'Our apologies for our absence,' he started, without taking his eyes off her. 'Odessa and I were getting...reacquainted.'

His tone dripped with deliberate innuendo and he didn't regret it one bit. Tugging her even closer, he captured her hand in his and raised it to his lips. Catching her shocked inhalation, he allowed his lips to curve, his eyes to grow hooded as they raked her flushed face.

Then he levelled his gaze once more on the mourners. 'While this isn't the venue I would've chosen, we're too impatient and eager to keep the news to ourselves.'

'What news?' Flávio demanded, his eyes flaming with a mix of speculation, anger and greed.

Ares let the suspense linger for a few seconds, then he

gripped her hands tighter. 'That your lovely niece has just accepted my proposal. Odessa and I are to be married. As soon as possible.'

Oh, God. Oh, God. *Oh, God.*

Light-headedness assaulted Odessa as Ares's announcement dropped like flaming hailstones on her.

He'd just…just announced—

She'd done it!

She tucked her free hand behind her back and dug her fingers into her palm to test if she was still awake. The sting registered firmly enough to reassure her that, yes, she was indeed conscious.

Somehow, by some miracle, her bold and wild gamble had paid off.

*But at what cost?*

Because his firm grip on her waist and that silkily drawled warning about keeping her word, that hard look in his eyes and the tension in his body despite the charming smile he was displaying…

Everything indicated strongly that Ares Zanelis wasn't coming to her aid out of the goodness of his heart. Hell, his initial cold *no* still resonated like distant thunder in her ears.

A formidable reckoning was headed her way—one she didn't fool herself into thinking wouldn't exact a crushing toll.

She knew it in her bones.

And as hushed whispers swelled into rushed speculation she was left in no doubt at all that she'd truly set the cat among the pigeons.

*But at least she'd evaded Vincenzo and her uncle's clutches.*

As frying pans and fires compared, she'd take that outcome. For now.

She pushed the harrowing thoughts away as Ares leaned

in close, his lips almost brushing her earlobe, and another cascade of shivers crashed through her body, reminding her in vivid colour of how she'd reacted to that kiss.

Dear God, she'd allowed him to kiss her—heck, she'd all but fallen into his decadent kiss—*at her father's funeral.*

'I know you're in mourning, but try for a small smile at least, *agapita.* This was your idea, after all, and you've just been granted your heart's desire. Act like it.'

She couldn't refute that. So Odessa forced lips that still tingled and stung from his voracious kiss to curve. Forced herself to focus as the crowd surged towards her, morbid curiosity driving them forward.

She was almost thankful when Ares raised his hand, halting the advancing guests.

'Please respect that my fiancée is mourning her father. If you wish us well, we accept gratefully, but I'm sure you'll understand that she'd like to conclude this occasion as originally scheduled before discussing any new matters.'

Her heart thudded wildly when he lifted her hand and brushed his lips across it once more.

Then he was urging her across the room—not towards her uncle, but to where his father stood, a pleased smile on his face.

Sergios grasped her free hand the moment she was within touching distance, a joyful light glinting in his eyes. 'My dear, let me be the first to welcome you to our family. You have no idea how happy you've made an old man.'

Her startled gaze flew to Ares. The clear caution in his eyes stilled her tongue, but inside a shrill voice screamed. She blinked in surprise and alarm when she saw the film of tears in the old man's laughing eyes. And as he turned to address his son in rapid-fire Greek cold waves of consternation washed over her.

*What had she done?*

She hadn't considered the old man's feelings when she'd hatched her desperate plot. The thought of upsetting him settled over her like a suffocating cloak making it hard to breathe. Was it too late to—

'No room for regret now, *eros mou*,' Ares rasped in her ear, eerily and accurately dissecting her thoughts.

His ominous words reverberated through her head in the hour it took for the funeral to conclude. They grew even louder when they were finally alone with Flávio, Vincenzo and a handful of distant relatives.

Sergios had gone to see the butler's much talked about newborn grandson—a move she suspected had been orchestrated by Ares. And now her heart stuttered for a different reason as Vincenzo strode towards him, fury blazing in his eyes as they shifted from her and settled on Ares.

'I don't know who you think you are—'

'Were we not introduced properly?' Ares interrupted coolly, pivoting to face Vincenzo, who was at least a foot shorter and was made to feel every millimetre of it when Ares peered down from his great height. 'Let me correct the oversight. I'm Ares Zanelis, Odessa's betrothed. And you are…?' he drawled, his tone sounding bored in the extreme.

The older man spluttered in outrage before spinning towards her uncle. 'Flávio, inform this little upstart who I am, will you?'

'This is Vincenzo Bartorelli. A…a business acquaintance,' her uncle stated.

Odessa, breath held, waited to hear her what else her uncle would add. To her shock, Flávio's gaze caught Ares's. A pointed look passed between the men, clearly fully deciphered by Vincenzo. His beady eyes narrowed and his fingers tightened around his glass until she feared it would shatter.

'You will all regret this,' Vincenzo snarled, encompassing Flávio, Ares and her in his look.

A cold shiver danced down her spine, but Ares shrugged off the threat. 'I doubt it sincerely.'

Vincenzo's livid stare switched to Flávio, who pretended interest in the contents of his glass. With a thick curse loaded with venom, Vincenzo turned on his heel and stormed out.

The ensuing silence was broken by Flávio's throat-clearing. 'Now that's settled, it would be remiss of me not to express my own concerns. At the very least I would've hoped to be asked for my niece's hand before you made the announcement.'

Ares's jaw clenched. 'Pretending to be old-fashioned when it suits your purposes isn't a great look on you. You have a price. We'll discuss it while my fiancée packs her bags.'

Alarm and rebellion ignited in her belly. 'What? I'm not leaving—'

'You wish to stay here?' Ares breathed, his eyes glinting cynicism.

No, she admitted reluctantly. She didn't. But she hadn't anticipated a cataclysmic move so soon. And while a part of her swelled with relief, a disconcerted part couldn't help but wonder what came next for her.

Because they hadn't even discussed what he expected in return for helping her. Considering the circumstances of their parting ten years ago, would it be as intolerable as her current situation?

Her stomach churned with something that skated past terror and into charged excitement. And then apprehension. What if she couldn't fulfil her part?

'Odessa?'

'I...I do need a little time to pack.'

Ares raised a cold eyebrow at her uncle.

Flávio shrugged. 'Certain wheels are already set in motion and will take considerable effort to halt,' he said. But with a quick glance at Ares's set face he hurriedly added,

'But I anticipate it all going smoothly since we both only have your best interests at heart.'

She barely stopped herself from snorting. Just this morning he'd intended to follow her father's wishes and barter her to a man over twice her age without so much as a by-your-leave. A man he knew to be cruel and violent.

Her sore wrist tingled. She rubbed at it absently, then tensed when Ares's gaze dropped to follow the action, his face tightening.

'Let's get this over with,' he grated at Flávio.

To his credit, her uncle obviously sensed the capriciousness of Ares's mood and nodded immediately. She watched them stride to the door, her breath shortening as she took in Ares's imposing form.

Every ounce of the playfulness of the man she'd known a decade ago had disappeared, leaving behind a breathtakingly formidable man whose presence made her breath catch.

He turned without warning at the door, catching her staring. A layer of tightness evaporated, and whatever he saw on her face drew a ghost of a smile.

'You have one hour. No more.'

One hour to leave her old life behind.

Odessa walked through her bedroom, wasting time she didn't have in trailing her fingers over possessions she'd never grown attached to. As a crime boss, her father had insisted on his daughter keeping up appearances, which had meant wearing the right in-season clothes and jewellery, and hanging out with the daughters of other influential and powerful men on the rare occasions he'd allowed her out.

But the very idea of being on display all the time—an undertaking she remembered her mother hating—had long ago become a chore she'd taken no pleasure in.

So she picked up and set down objects she wouldn't miss, her open suitcase on the bed still mostly empty a long while later.

'You're not packed?'

She whirled around at the drawl from her open doorway. Had the hour passed already? She glanced down at her watch, a diamond and platinum Cartier gifted to her by her father in a lavish display of ostentation at her birthday party two years ago. As usual it had come with a price—this one a dinner date with the son of a burgeoning rival her father had wanted mollified.

She'd failed, her fierce rebellion against being used as a pawn fuelling her defiance. He hadn't been happy.

She saw Ares catch her shudder at the memory, and preempted an interrogation by replying, 'Not quite yet.'

He glanced around the room, disdain staining his face. 'That's good. Because you will bring nothing with you. Including that.' He nodded at the watch.

Surprise stiffened her spine, despite her having had the same thought a minute ago. 'What?'

'Tell me there's anything here that you're remotely attached to?' he challenged coolly.

She wanted to protest, but secretly she was relieved to leave it all behind. Everything here signified oppression under her father's ruthless thumb.

*But aren't you exchanging one version of hell for another? This man shattered your dreams...left you behind.*

No, this path was of her own choosing. And while Ares had gained a ruthless reputation, he hadn't turned cruel, had he?

'What is it?'

She started, and realised she'd been examining him with rabid intent. Was it to see if he wore his cruelty as proudly as her father had worn his?

'Odessa?'

'I'm wondering if you'll be as cruel to me as my father was,' she confessed brazenly.

She was done with walking innocently into situations, trusting as blindly as she'd trusted him years ago. It was the only way she could guard her emotions. After all, if she wasn't pinning any foolish hopes on him she couldn't be disappointed, could she?

He stiffened, his expression growing remote. Within a heartbeat he was sliding his fingers into her hair, tilting her face up so he could spear her with outraged eyes. 'You dare compare me to that monster?' he seethed.

Her heart squeezed. 'I thought I knew you…back then. But it turned out I was wrong, so who knows?'

'*You* do. You just choose to misremember. To make yourself feel better by pretending what's happening to you right now is entirely everyone else's fault when you must bear some responsibility.'

'That's not true. I've just learned that nothing stays the same. People change. The evidence is standing right before me.'

His eyes gleamed, as if he found her amusing and infuriating all at once. Then, just as quickly, his expression hardened. 'No, people don't change. Sometimes they just hide who they are until it suits them to reveal themselves. Other times the people in their lives just choose not to notice.'

He meant her, of course.

Odessa bit her lip, felt the urge to explain herself, to explain Paolo and *that kiss* stalking through her. But before she could fabricate the words he swung away, impatience bristling in his towering frame. Just as he'd turned away that night. Only he hadn't just turned away. He'd seized the role of judge, jury and executioner, and then abandoned her without a backward glance.

*Remember that!*

'It's time to go, Odessa.'

Not without some assurances.

'My uncle—'

'Is not going to be a problem,' he said, jaw tight.

A spike of anguish lanced her. 'Should I ask how many silver shekels I was sold for?'

'No. It's not important,' he rasped.

She wanted to scream that it was to her. But she knew she'd just be furthering her heartache. She'd been a pawn for every power-hungry member of her family her entire life.

*But no more.*

She raised her chin and caught a flash of something in his eyes almost like surprise…admiration. But then he was slanting an impatient glance at his watch.

She went to her bedside drawer. Opening it, she took out her most treasured item. Her mother's locket. It held the only picture she had of Renata Santella. Her father had disposed of everything else in a fit of drunken pique soon after her mother had died. Odessa had been conveniently out of the house. It was one of the many things she'd never forgiven him for.

She sensed Ares wandering close. 'You still have that?' he enquired gruffly.

She cradled the delicate locket in her hand. 'Some things are worth hanging on to. No matter what.'

Unsure why she'd said that, she caught her breath as she glanced up, saw the ghost of a prickling gentleness—because this man would never be *completely* soft—before his expression hardened once more.

They stayed like that for charged seconds before he pivoted away, leaving her to breathe freely again, to pick up the credit card holding the five thousand euros her mother had been able to secrete away and pass to Odessa to keep for a desperate rainy day.

It was definitely torrential today. And petrifying. Because she was still in the dark about the price to be paid for Ares freeing her.

'Are you done?'

The query was gruff, but not impatient. Why, she couldn't tell, because his face was back to being coolly distant.

A pair of jeans, a few tops, shoes and two changes of underwear packed, she snapped the case shut.

She wasn't surprised when Ares took hold of it with one hand, his other circling her elbow as he guided her out.

Her heart lurched, then thumped, when she saw Flávio waiting in the grand hall, a false smile playing at his lips even as his eyes continued to assess her keenly, searching to see if she'd done anything to ruin whatever he'd extracted from Ares.

She knew the moment he realised he'd succeeded in whatever deal he'd struck.

He came towards her, arms wide open.

Under the pretext of kissing his niece goodbye, he whispered in Italian. 'You've surprised me, niece. I didn't think you'd manage to pull a stunt like this. *Brava.* You're a true Santella after all. But don't forget where you came from. And remember... I'll be watching.'

'What did he say to you?' Ares asked after they'd stepped out into the late-autumn sunshine.

She shook her head, eager to forget Flávio's threat. 'It doesn't matter.'

Now it was happening, she wanted to get away from here immediately. More importantly, she wanted to ask Ares where he was taking her, what he wanted from her.

But he was ushering her down the steps to where a gleaming limousine waited, with a sharply dressed driver holding the back door open. Ares grasped her hand lightly and helped her in, then he followed.

Odessa looked around in surprise as the driver shut the door and hurried to settle behind the wheel. 'Isn't your father coming with us?'

A hard smile twitched his lips as the engine started. 'He is.'

When he didn't expand, she glanced out of the window, then realised they were driving away from the main house, heading towards the servants' quarters. Where he and his father used to live. Where the other staff members including the butler still lived.

The vehicle rounded a curve and stopped in front of the garages.

Odessa had avoided this part of the estate in recent years, mostly due to the man who now sat next to her.

It was in the orange grove beyond the servants' quarters that Ares had kissed her for the first time. Where he'd touched her, whispered sultry Greek words in her ear she hadn't understood, and made her dream the impossible.

After his departure she'd been unable to return here, the memories too painful. Plus, her father had threatened all the servants against entertaining her near their quarters, mistakenly believing that they'd colluded in her secret liaison with the chauffeur's son. It had been better for everyone that she stayed away.

Now the memories rushed at her, so fast and furious she clenched her fingers in her lap.

'Haunted by your demons, *agapita*?' he rasped.

She tightened her grip on her composure. 'My demons? What about yours? Or does the great Ares Zanelis not have any?'

'Hmm, you've got better at deflecting…but it still doesn't answer me.'

About to snap back with a sharp retort, she stopped as Sergios emerged, the butler following behind with his grandson cradled lovingly in his arms. Beside her, Ares tensed, his focus fixed on his father.

Inscrutable expressions twitched across his face. Odessa didn't know why they sent trepidation dancing down her spine.

She pushed it away as a clutch of staff approached the limo. Ares watched with narrow-eyed intent when she stepped out and was immediately engulfed in hugs and whispers of farewell, well wishes that made her chest squeeze in shame. But looking into their faces she saw understanding, and—surprisingly—encouragement.

Odessa sucked in a breath when she sensed Ares behind her. He muttered in Greek to his father. The older man nodded impatiently then, turning to the newborn, brushed stiff fingers over the child's cheek, a wistful yearning crossing his face before his trademark smile returned.

As they returned to the car she caught the look of deep introspection on Ares's face as his gaze lingered on his father.

And once again a heavy tingling took hold of her nape.

# CHAPTER THREE

'WHERE ARE WE GOING?' Odessa kept her gaze fixed ahead, her poise admirable as they drove through the absurdly ostentatious gilded gates that guarded the entrance to the Santella estate.

It was a reasonable question, and Ares was surprised she hadn't asked before now, but now that she had it irritated him a little. He wanted to ask why she cared. Surely anywhere else on earth was better than what she'd just left behind.

He wondered if she would've lobbied any other man for opportunistic deliverance if he hadn't been present.

The very idea shot icy repugnance through his gut.

From the corner of his eye he watched her nurse her sore wrist, anger and that spurt of disquieting protectiveness unsettling him all over again. He tightened his fist, stamping out the urge to take her hand in his, to soothe the bruise. For one thing, his father's speculative glance was growing heavier by the minute.

While he mostly confided heavily in his father, he was curiously reluctant to divulge his innermost thoughts to his parent just now.

Perhaps because he still wasn't sure just what his intention was? Or because the very idea of it unnerved him in the extreme and yet he couldn't rid himself of it?

He shifted in his seat, eager to dislodge the knot that had

anchored itself to his chest, resisting the urge to grit his teeth when it refused to budge.

'We're flying to Rome,' he answered eventually. 'I have business to take care of there tomorrow. Then we're heading home to Athens. After that...we'll see.'

Eyes widening a touch, she nodded serenely, her posture almost regal. 'Okay, but...' She paused, her gaze darting to Sergios.

Ares knew why she'd hesitated, and was glad of his father's presence. It bought him time to deliberate over this rash decision. To decide whether the prime piece of real estate in Porto Novo he'd handed over to Flávio Santella—warehouses worth two million euros—was worth the headache he'd just landed himself with. Quite apart from that, and more concerningly, the absurd, unconscionable notion that had rocked him just now was one he needed distance from as quickly as possible.

'We'll discuss the details later...when we're all rested.'

Irritation sparked across her face, curiously making him want to laugh. True, he wasn't usually one to crave rest with deals waiting to be made—especially when it was barely mid-afternoon. He'd closed more deals in the hours between when most people clocked off for the day and midnight than he could count. But he wasn't about to dissect his decision now.

He watched her glance out of the window, then shift her whole body until she was looking through the rear-view mirror at the gaudy, oppressive mansion where she'd grown up.

Before he could stop himself, he cupped her chin, redirected her focus to his. 'No looking back,' he said. 'You will look forward from now on.'

He'd meant it as an order, yet it emerged gruff and low, as if infusing her with a strength he didn't owe her. And, like in the bedroom, her wide silver eyes darted to his and held. The punch those eerily beautiful eyes packed sent an alarming jolt through him.

He removed his touch before he did something insane… like caress her smooth skin one more time.

He'd done enough of that today.

His father's smug look once she'd faced forward sent tingles through Ares's body. Tingles he ignored, thankful that Sergios, for whatever reason, was choosing discretion over his usual exuberance. But he couldn't forget the vehemence with which Sergios had demanded to come to Elio's funeral, his eagerness to search out his ex-boss's daughter.

The journey to the private airport was thankfully short, but the breath of fresh air when he stepped out did nothing to uncoil his tension or remove Odessa's alluring fragrance from his senses.

He stalked away towards his plane, leaving his father chatting to her as he boarded. Choosing a solo armchair, he drew out his phone and busied himself with business as they took off and winged their way towards the Italian capital.

Ares knew his tension wasn't making things better, but he couldn't help himself.

*Thee mou*, it grated to remember that he'd never been able to help himself all those years ago, when infatuation had led him down a dangerous path. But he was his own man now.

And this time she would dance to *his* tune.

Two hours later, he stopped out of the shower in the penthouse suite at the Bella Regenciana on Via Labicana. The iconic building that overlooked the Colosseum held a particular significance to him. It'd been the first substantial deal he'd lost to a more ruthless competitor when he'd first tried to acquire it. Five years later he'd bought it for cents on the euro, when the greedy, severely over-extended mogul had lost everything.

These days he was used to having the last laugh.

He didn't feel like laughing when he entered his bedroom and saw his father lounging on the plush sofa opposite the bed.

Ares stifled a groan. 'What are you doing here? You should be resting.'

'Ah, this "resting" thing seems to be going around a lot today.'

He cringed at his father's air quotes.

'Is there something on your mind, Baba?'

'I'm more concerned about what's on yours,' Sergios replied.

He could pretend he didn't know what his father was talking about, but they'd long passed that stage of their relationship. They'd needed to stop hiding behind walls and façades a long time ago, when rejection, cruelty and grief had bound them together in an unbreakable bond.

Decades later, Ares still couldn't stem the searing pain when he thought of his two-year-old sister Sofia and the mother who'd selfishly broken their family apart. Her last resort—claiming Sofia wasn't his father's—had been particularly cruel, a vicious retaliation for her husband's supposed neglect.

It hadn't mattered to her that Sergios had been bending over backwards to give her the life she craved. Or that Elio Santella was a devilish taskmaster who'd demanded unreasonable loyalty. His mother's unhappiness had unfolded in the worst possible way, starting with her desertion and ending in tragedy.

Her death a mere six months later in a fiery car crash, along with Sofia and her new lover, had almost destroyed Sergios, and Ares knew he'd never forgiven himself for the mistakes he'd made.

Ares had grown up knowing his father wanted more than

one child. And Sergios had been overcome with grief at losing the daughter he'd barely had a chance to know. But he'd buried it for Ares's sake.

Ares had never forgotten that.

But, as much as he was still to decide on the final outcome of his actions, he didn't want his father disillusioned. The old man had suffered enough at his mother's hands.

'I know it seems sudden, but I know what I'm doing,' he said.

Sergios's brows rose. 'Do you?'

Ares strode towards his dressing room, avoiding his father's stare. 'If you're concerned about how things have turned out today, don't be.'

'Oh, I'm not. On the contrary, I think she's perfect for you,' his father mused.

Ares stiffened, and a punch of something closely resembling panic slammed into his gut as that tingling from earlier returned. 'Was that why you insisted on attending the funeral? Because you'd hoped for this outcome?'

'What outcome?' Sergios returned, his eyes probing deeper. 'Are you referring to the unfinished business between you two? The thing that's been holding you back from true happiness?'

Hot and cold chills danced over him as the weight of those words pressed down on him.

'True happiness is a myth,' he growled. 'And no one's perfect, Baba. You know that.'

He kicked himself for the flash of pain that flitted across Sergios's face at the despised reminder that they'd both been deserted in the cruellest way possible, and then visited with unspeakable tragedy while they'd still been licking their wounds.

Ares's fingers gripped the cotton shirt he'd plucked from a hanger, his thoughts rearing back in time, even though he didn't need any mental gymnastics to work out that his sister would've been turning thirty this year if she'd lived.

Silence thickened behind him as he dressed, then pressed more heavily when he returned to the bedroom, his cufflinks in his palm. 'I know what I'm doing, Baba. And please don't get your hopes up, okay?' he implored.

His father stared at him through unusually pensive eyes. Then he rose. He stopped long enough to tap Ares lightly on his hard cheek, then headed for the door.

'You're a strong powerful man, but even you can't stop me from hoping, *yios*. For both our sakes, don't make the same mistakes I did.'

Ares's tension remained long after the door had shut behind his father…long after he'd secured the cufflinks and shrugged on his jacket.

He was straining to switch himself into business mode when he stepped into the living room and saw her on the terrace. She'd changed into a pair of jeans that did infuriatingly delicious things to her backside and her long, shapely legs. From this angle he couldn't ignore the way her top moulded firm, high breasts and a flat stomach, or the fact that her hair was down, skimming her lower back and almost touching those firm globes.

He'd felt that heavy mass of lustrous curls more than once…knew the very real temptation it held for a man to bury his fists in it. To draw those curls to his nose and luxuriate in her scent. To picture those tresses spread across his pillow.

Ares cursed under his breath when his body rudely awakened. He took an involuntary step towards her before he caught himself.

No, his misguided moments of dancing to this princess's tune were in his past.

Reversing direction with another pithy curse, he exited the penthouse, his father's words ringing in his ears.

The first morning of her freedom.

Odessa stood on the balcony; her face raised to the sun.

Like yesterday evening, the air smelled fresh and crisp, with a tang of lemons that drew a smile. The distinct absence of a sea breeze pressed home the fact that she was no longer in Alghero. That her bold strike had succeeded in removing her from under her uncle's thumb. That, despite the unanswered questions hanging over her head, she'd slept more soundly than she could ever remember sleeping.

'Enjoying your liberation?'

She tensed, then turned around to find Ares lounging against the door.

Despite it being barely seven o'clock, he was dressed in formal business attire, his clean-shaven jaw and the slight sheen to his hair drawing attention to his chiselled face.

The espresso cup in his hand next drew her gaze to his long, elegant fingers. Her breath shortened, her traitorous body rousing in appreciation of the virile, sophisticated picture he made.

Odessa gripped the railing tighter to ground herself. 'Enjoying the morning air, *si*.'

His gaze lingered. The thundercloud of displeasure he'd exhibited during their plane ride from Alghero to Rome had seemingly dissipated sometime between their arrival at the hotel and now. Her next breath came easier, because while squaring off with him was strangely invigorating, she welcomed the respite.

'Have you ever been to Rome?' he asked, almost conversationally, stepping onto the terrace.

She shook her head. 'Capri for the summer still remains the extent of my travels. Until now, at least.'

Capri was where her father had decreed that the family would vacation. He hadn't liked going where he wasn't known, or where he couldn't effectively lord his status over everyone else. During her late teens she'd been constrained, when most women her age, with the kind of means she'd grown up with, would have been exploring the world. His grip had only tightened in the years after Ares left, with her heartbroken defiance sealing her fate.

She swallowed down the rising bitterness.

As if Ares sensed her thoughts, his lips firmed. A second later he threw back his beverage and set the cup and saucer down on a nearby table.

'The day is yours. Feel free to explore. We'll go out to dinner tonight. Rome at night is not as special as Athens, but it's still quite spectacular.'

Her grip tightened. She knew she couldn't succumb to the awed sensation attempting to sweep her away. There was a catch. There was *always* a catch.

'You didn't bring me here to play tourist. Are you going to tell me what you want in return for helping me or is it going to hang over my head like the sword of Damocles?'

He strolled closer, his hands sliding into his pockets. The movement threw the breadth of his shoulders into relief, inviting attention to the muscle play beneath his shirt.

'I thought we already settled that, *agapita*? We're getting married.'

Her jaw dropped, and then, after the tiniest wild agitation, her heart along with it. 'But that's… *No.* You just said that yesterday to throw Uncle Flávio and Vincenzo off. It was never meant to be real. I was thinking more along the lines of a fake engagement for a while, maybe a few months, then calling it off…' Her words trailed off when his expression grew sardonic.

'Were you?' he drawled.

Heat filled her face. 'Don't mock me, Ares.'

His amusement evaporated. 'And don't presume you have any power to dictate how things proceed. You handed that over, remember?'

'Actually, no. I didn't.' She swallowed the knot in her throat. 'I said anything you want. Not everything,' she ventured, even while that *'we're getting married'* continued to ping wild desires through her blood.

*Santo cielo,* what she wouldn't have given to hear that years ago. *But it was a pipe dream. Remember that...*

He stared at her for a short stretch before glancing down at his watch. 'I'm going to be late for my meeting. You'll have the day to yourself, but be ready to go out when I return at seven.' He started to turn, then paused. 'Make no mistake, *agapita.* You will marry me, as per your request. And you will also give me that *anything I want.'*

She watched him leave, her insides a sickening mess of wild agitation and shock.

Ares wanted to marry her?

*Why?*

It sure as hell wasn't because he wanted her. He'd stated plainly yesterday that he wasn't there for her. And hadn't he responded with a cold hard *no* when she'd first made the ludicrously hopeful suggestion?

What on earth could've changed between then and now to make him want this? Surely not the *kiss*?

Questions dogged her, sending her pacing through her suite after breakfast with Sergios. He tried to coax her into going for a walk with him afterwards, but she was too riled up about his son's announcement to be tempted to stretch the boundaries of her freedom for the first time.

Her rollercoaster of agitation only intensified when the concierge rang at four p.m. to say there was a couturier heading up to the penthouse. The elegantly dressed middle-aged woman swept in with two assistants, one tugging a gold porter's trolley bearing three sleek garments bags and boxes of matching accessories, and the other carrying a large case that turned out to contain the very best in luxury make-up.

The folded note bearing her name attached to one garment bag was short and succinct.

*Choose a gown. I prefer the red. A*

On the heels of spending hours in the grip of confusion, Odessa's first knee-jerk reaction was rebellion. And that spurt of rebellion hardened when the garment turned out to be a sleeveless floor-length blood-red satin sheath with a plunging neckline and no back at all.

Heat flared in her cheeks as she imagined herself in it with no underwear—because there was no way she could pull off wearing panties, never mind a bra, in this dress.

*'Diavolo, no!'* she snapped under breath, ignoring the looks that passed between the other women.

Thrusting it aside, she reached for the next bag, somewhat mollified when she saw an off-white dress. It was better, but still a little too risqué, with its thigh-high slit and geometric gaps beneath the bust and at the hipline. She wasn't in the mood to show so much of her midriff and hipbones, thank you very much.

The last garment made her exhale in relief.

Ice-blue, with a waterfall skirt in soft chiffon, the halter neck design would leave her arms free in the cool early autumn air, and while a slit in the back negated wearing a bra, it was still tasteful enough that she reached eagerly for it.

'This one.'

The couturier snapped her fingers. Within minutes, matching accessories had been laid out. A quick shower later, and she was in front of the mirror in her dressing room, the experts barely intruding as her hair was blow-dried, curled and styled in an up-do with tendrils framing her face. The make-up accentuating her eyes in dark and silver shadow was understated, and yet dramatic enough to make Odessa's mouth gape in astonishment.

All three women gushed compliments, and once her dress, shoes and clutch bag were in place, they were spirited away as dramatically as they'd arrived.

It wasn't the first time she'd dressed up to meet a man. Her father had paired her up and dangled her in front of friends' sons and acquaintances more times than she could count. But this was the first time she'd dressed for Ares Zanelis. And as much as she despised the nerves chewing her up, she couldn't stem them.

She rose from the sofa when he entered, and watched him grind to a halt, his eyes wide with something heavy and profound that restarted the rollercoaster all over again. She withstood his intense scrutiny, feeling every second of the thorough, almost obsessive head-to-toe inspection, and his utter fascination with looking into her eyes.

She knew the make-up made her eyes look saucer-wide and almost haunting, but…

'If you're going to make a big deal about me not wearing the red dress, save your breath. I'd rather wear nothing at all than wear that *thing.*'

She only realised what she'd blurted a moment later and groaned under her breath.

Ares prowled closer, his fingers undoing his suit jacket before he shrugged it off. Odessa hated it that she had to fight to drag her gaze away from the chiselled perfection he revealed.

'Is that so? Well, far be it for me to subject the public to the scandalous spectacle of your nakedness.'

The smile teasing his lips sparked a suspicion that drew a gasp. 'The red wasn't your real choice at all, was it?'

His amusement deepened and she knew she'd been played.

'I suspected you would want to show your claws. You always were your fiercest when given an order.'

The recollection of him saying something similar years ago landed sharp and raw between them, making her pulse race. But his amusement evaporated a second later, indicating that he hadn't meant to bring that up. Hadn't meant to share that memory with her.

'I'll be ready in fifteen minutes,' he clipped out, then strode off, leaving her stomach churning once again.

She'd barely got her runaway pulse and scattering senses to calm when he returned. His business suit had been swapped for a black dinner jacket and matching trousers with a thin strip of black satin down the side seam that accentuated his lean athleticism. The first few buttons of his midnight-blue silk shirt were undone, baring his strong throat and the faintest wisps of chest hair.

Odessa was immediately thrown back to a younger Ares, rising out of the sea after an illicit midnight swim. Even back then she'd been in complete girlish awe over his chiselled form. Now every womanly cell in her body heated at the erotic sight of all that raw male perfection, barely restrained by the trappings of sophistication.

'Shall we?' he rasped.

Blinking to drive away the lascivious thoughts, she glanced past him. 'Is Sergios not coming with us?'

He shook his head. 'No. He needs to rest. Besides, this evening is just for you and me.'

She wasn't going to apply any deeper meaning to that. He'd all but said outright this morning that he'd be finally stating his demands.

Her insides continued to twist into knots as he ushered her into the lift. Strained silence ticked between them, with Odessa grasping and discarding subjects she'd once been able to freely discuss with this man who was a complete stranger to her now.

She stepped out in relief when the doors opened—relief which was immediately shattered when he caught her hand in a light hold.

She glanced up and saw the pointed look in his eyes.

Right. To the outside world, they were getting married. Because she'd asked him and, for soon-to-be-disclosed reasons, he'd obliged.

And now what? They must pretend to be happily about to be engaged?

She swallowed a snort before it could escape, eager to get outside, where hopefully a dose of fresh air would clear her head. But awaiting them were eager staff who jumped when they saw him coming, hotel guests who eyed them with wide-eyed speculation, and the latest model Ferrari supercar idling kerbside. She knew it was worth over a million, because Flávio had greedily and openly coveted it for the last six months.

Sliding in, she felt her senses immediately latch on to Ares's unique scent, seemingly imprinted in the space. It only intensified when he dropped into the bucket seat beside her, his large frame shrinking the interior until it felt as if he was all she could see, all she could breathe.

In a wild bid to dissipate the charged atmosphere she revisited the subject they'd skimmed minutes ago, as Ares gunned the engine and accelerated into the Rome night.

'What you said about Sergios… Is he all right? Did the accident—'

'How do you know about that?' he demanded sharply, his body stiffening.

'We have TVs in Alghero, you know. Besides, I could hardly miss it. You seem to be a big deal these days.'

He eased the car into the road, the clench-unclench of his thighs playing in the strobe of passing streetlights. 'Am I?'

'Self-effacing doesn't become you.'

A layer of tension released and the corner of his lips quirked. 'You'll be hard pressed to find anything that *becomes* me, *agapita*,' he murmured evenly, but she heard a slight bite behind the statement.

She wondered again what had been involved in his meteoric rise to the top in just a short decade. Before she could ask, he was continuing.

'My father likes to pretend he'll live for ever. And as much as I'd like that...'

His lips pursed and she saw a flash of bleakness that was stark and stomach-hollowing under the next passing streetlight.

'They discovered a heart condition during his recovery.'

Her heart squeezed. 'I'm...I'm sorry. Is it serious?'

He remained silent for a tight stretch. 'Most heart conditions are—especially at his age.'

It was said in a finite way that didn't invite more speculation or questions. But she was reluctant to return to the charged silence...reluctant to probe her own feelings too closely.

'And you? You were in a coma for a while.'

She felt his probing gaze when he pulled up at a traffic light.

'You were paying attention that much, *agapita*?'

That edge was present in his tone, but there was something else. Surprise? Curiosity? The tiniest softening? Or was it wishful thinking?

'No matter what happened between us, I never wished you ill, Ares.'

His chest moved and her heart lifted with...hope? But his lips had tightened again.

'That's good, because in the telling of our brief story you would've been hard pressed to come out the victim at any point.'

Her insides twisted hard, but she pushed the anguish away. 'I don't think of myself as a victim. But neither am I a villain. Our past is—'

'In the past,' he interrupted. 'Tonight is about what comes next for you and me.'

Before she could respond, Ares was pulling up in front of one of the many centuries-old buildings the city was known for. It looked nondescript from the outside, but even its act of attempting to look plain hinted at hidden delights.

She wasn't mistaken.

The moment Ares alighted, a smartly dressed young man approached, took his car keys, and waved them through the ordinary-looking doors.

After a dozen steps on a black carpet they came to dramatic red double doors and a stone-paved corridor lit with large medieval fire lamps thrust into the walls high above their heads. It was so evocative of a bygone era that she stared around her, her mouth agape.

'Where are we?'

'Teatro Romana di Caracalla. A private exclusive theatre owned by a friend. It was a rundown apartment building when I sold it to him two years ago. He's turned it around admirably. At any other time I would've preferred for us to have the place to ourselves, but tonight calls for a curated audience.'

Her breath snagged in her chest. 'What's special about tonight?'

One eyebrow arched in a satirical mockery. 'You do want the message reinforced, don't you? Or would you rather leave Bartorelli with the impression that he still has a chance?'

A cold shudder went through her. 'No, I wouldn't.'

'Good.'

He tugged her hand onto his sleeve and escorted her to the end of the corridor, which opened up into a wide balcony. Below the balcony a semi-circular theatre was set out not with rows of seats but with twelve semi-circular dining tables with chairs facing the stage. The whole theatre rose three storeys high, with more fire torches fixed along the walls up to the ceiling.

It was spectacular, and she would've loved to explore, had Ares's intentions not been uppermost in her thoughts.

He led her to a table clearly set out centre stage, briefly acknowledging the occupants of the other tables. Odessa was keenly aware that they were the cynosure of every pair of eyes, and murmurs of interest were flaring.

Vintage champagne set in a silver bucket was poured into crystal flutes as the lights went down. Then the first haunting strings of a familiar opera drew fresh tingles down her spine.

Her gaze darted to Ares. *'Tristan and Isolde?'*

A ghost of a smile drifted over his lips as he clinked his glass against hers. 'Your favourite story, *ne*?'

Her breath caught. 'You remember?'

'The curse of having a steel trap memory,' he said with a throwaway shrug, his face shuttered in a way that made her heart drop.

The first act of the twisted, heart-tugging love story was accompanied by a superb lobster salad and then sublime gnocchi, salmon and truffle cheese served by unobtrusive attendants trained in the art of melting into the background.

By the time the lights came up on first intermission, Odessa's emotions were threatening to strangle her. The reasons behind Ares choosing an opera that celebrated a fierce forbidden love that ended in tragedy had triggered higher emotions and put her on fierce alert.

Was it a metaphor for them? A warning against reading anything into his actions?

Her gaze dropped to the table, to the expensive-looking square velvet box he was sliding across the table, and a loud gasp erupted through her jagged emotions. 'This is… You can't—'

'Open it,' he commanded, and there was a hoarse roughness to his voice despite his carefully neutral expression.

Her brain shrieked at her not to, but that foolish sliver of a doe-eyed girl lurking deep within her compelled her to reach out a trembling hand.

The blush-pink diamond was surrounded with two rows of tiny, flawless cushion-cut white diamonds mounted on a platinum base and narrow band, each one glinting and sparkling beneath the candlelight.

A gasp echoed somewhere to her right, and within a minute wild applause broke out, their audience cunningly pulled into this seemingly euphoric moment.

On cue, Ares rose, closed the gap between them, lifted the ring from its plush velvet cushion and slipped it onto her finger. All the while Odessa's mouth gaped in what might be construed as romantic shock but was in reality astonishment at how expertly she'd been played.

Under the pretext of brushing her lips with his—an act which left her mouth tingling and heat arrowing sharply between her legs—Ares took her chin in his hand, his eyes gleaming as he murmured, 'I would get down on one knee, but since we've been forced to put the cart before the horse I feel that moment has passed, no?'

Words failed her—both at the sheer magnificence of the ring and the image of Ares on one knee, playing out the secret impossible fantasy she'd harboured for far too long during her teenage years.

'When did you do this?' she asked, pushing away the

more pressing questions she wanted to blurt out. Like *why* he was pushing this ruse. Why was he going to such great lengths for something neither of them truly wanted?

*Are you sure?*

'Does it matter?' he drawled dismissively, as if a proposal that would've made an enormous swathe of women swoon was merely an item he'd ticked off his list tonight.

'You're right. It doesn't matter,' she forced out.

Theirs wasn't a reunion filled with breathless proclamations and the obsessive need to tabulate every single moment of their for ever pledge. She'd made a desperate request and he'd grudgingly obliged, with conditions of his own he'd yet to make fully known to her.

'Are we going to get the suspense over with now?' she rasped, aware that they were under even more intense scrutiny.

Hell, that diamond on her finger commanded an audience all its own.

He took his seat, and she noticed he'd moved much closer to her. With their table distanced from the other tables, they were out of eavesdropping range. The enforced proximity ramped up her tension, her stomach churning as he watched her for an age before he spoke the words she suspected would turn her life as she knew it inside out.

'In return for keeping you out of the clutches of your uncle and that bastard,' he started, his eyes glinting hard as his gaze dropped to the faint yellow marks on her wrist, 'you'll stay married to me for five years, or however long it takes for you to give me two children—minimum. If we're blessed with more in those five years, then they will be well received. After that, you'll be free to live your life however you want.'

# CHAPTER FOUR

IN THE DUMBFOUNDING seconds that followed his words—
words that should have arrived with cymbals and trumpets
and exploding fireworks, considering the impossible utter
insanity they evoked—Odessa fully grasped why Ares had
chosen to do this in public.

Just like with the proposal, he'd sought to contain her response. And, oh, was he clever in doing so…

Because she only managed to keep the predictable screech
of disbelief and outrage trapped in her throat by the most
valiant fight with her willpower.

The hooded look in his eyes said he knew it.

He watched with avid interest as her heart raced madly
and her hands bunched on the table, shaking with the force
of suppressed emotion and causing the ring to sparkle in its
mocking presence even brighter.

She felt the blood drain from her head and take her belly
along with it to her toes.

Her lips parted but no words emerged.

Was it even worth reacting to this absurdity? *Yes*, her
frantic senses screeched. Because the steely determination
in his face screamed that he was serious.

*Dio mio.*

'Before you express anything other than complete ecstasy at my request, remember our audience,' he warned under his breath.

'This is why you brought me here? To corner me so I couldn't tell you how utterly crazy you are?' she hissed.

Despite the twitch of his lips, his eyes remained deadly serious, without a trace of insanity. 'My reasons are exactly as I stated. You get to enjoy your favourite opera, be offered the requisite diamond ring, and more importantly get your unwanted suitor off your back. In return, I've stated my demands. That you find it insane doesn't change the fact that those are my wishes. If you want to continue this conversation elsewhere, I'll be happy to oblige.' He looked around, his eyes gleaming with triumph. 'I think we've satisfied our objectives.'

He finished speaking just as a rotund man with a booming voice who introduced himself simply as 'Armand' approached. He expressed congratulations in Italian, to which Ares responded, speaking in a perfect accent that reminded her he spoke her mother tongue fluently.

Somehow Odessa managed to smile and respond, to hold out her hand when his wife arrived to gush over the ring. In minutes, they were inundated with other well-wishers.

Ten minutes after that Ares was firmly but good-humouredly announcing that they were leaving to celebrate in private. Odessa was still reeling as he escorted her out to their waiting car.

'That should take care of the publicity side of things. Armand's wife alone will ensure our news spreads across the continent before morning.'

She turned on him, her heartbeat still roaring in her ears. 'You... Tell me you were joking back there!'

'No. I was not.'

'Ares...'

She saw him tense at the whisper of his name, his fingers tightening briefly around the steering wheel before he relaxed them.

'We will be married long enough for the two children I require to be born or for five years—whichever comes first,' he reiterated, his voice like rumbling boulders that dropped onto her shoulders. 'And they will be born in Greece,' he tossed in, as if geography mattered one iota when she was grappling with his ludicrous demand.

'If all you need is a womb for hire, why do you need marriage at all? Surrogates are a dime a dozen these days.'

A muscle rippled in his jaw for a moment before he rasped, 'Because I wish to do things properly. For my father's sake. I'm sure you remember he's old-school in most ways?'

It was the last thing she'd expected him to say and it robbed her of speech, right along with the shock of the moment before. Because in some baffling way it made sense.

'Right. I see.'

And she truly did. In father and son she'd witnessed an unbending devotion that had sparked both yearning and envy. It had been the model she'd based all the foundations of her relationship goals on. Still...

'Why go through this...subterfuge? Isn't he going to be upset when he finds out?'

Tension clearly still riding him, he zipped them through traffic for a full minute before he replied.

'He'll never find out. As far as he's concerned every aspect of this marriage will be real. If I remember correctly your acting skills are impressive. You'll do everything in your power to convince him that our reunion is real. And if...' He paused, a flash of something resembling bleakness darting across his face before he neutralised his expression. 'And when the time comes for us to separate, I'll break the news to him in a way that minimises the damage. Hopefully by then he will be too preoccupied with his grandchildren to care.'

'You don't need to count on any imaginary acting skills you think I possess. I'm not participating in this...sham. Not for one year. Never mind five...or...' She waved that absurd thought away, the layers of shocked pain settling over her shoulders like an unwanted cloak as her brain struggled to grasp the unthinkable scenario he was drawing up. 'Are you really okay with pulling the wool over his eyes like this?'

'The eventual benefits will far outweigh the means of achieving my goals. It's salutary advice you'll do well to apply to your own circumstances.'

She swallowed a bark of hysterical laughter before it leapt free. He was really serious about this.

'Why five years?'

'Because it's the right age for a child to relinquish dependence on an absent parent. Any later and the damage could be irreparable.'

'How do you know this?' she asked, and then stinging recollection made her inhale sharply. 'Your own mother left when you were seven,' she murmured, almost afraid of voicing the reason he was pushing for this. 'Is this about...? Do you wish your mother had left earlier?'

His expression morphed into granite. 'This isn't about me.'

Of course it was. His whole being screamed it. But Odessa wisely didn't belabour the point.

'So I give you a child...children...and we divorce in five years?' Why did the words sear a path of pain in her throat?

Fully expecting him to agree, she was stunned when he shook his head. 'No. We will stay married for a minimum of five years. But if...when you decide to leave, you will relinquish full custody of our children to me. We won't divorce until my father is…' He stopped, expelling his breath in a rush.

Again absurdly, considering the utter lunacy of this conversation, Odessa's heart cracked for him, sympathy filling spaces long left wanting and hollow. She didn't need him to spell it out. Her mother's passing might have happened long ago enough for her only to recall hazy moments with the woman forced to stay in her husband's shadow, but deep in her heart the pain of losing her parent lingered.

She pushed back the memories to find Ares watching her.

'Five years is also a good age to ensure a child's memories fade sooner rather than later,' he tossed in.

The pang was sharper this time, lancing hard enough to make her gasp. 'Ares, this is insane!'

'And yet these are my terms. Take it or leave it.'

It didn't even register that they'd returned to the hotel's underground car park until the silence pressed in on her. The finality of his statement battered at any hope of getting him to rethink this streak of insanity, but she wasn't about to be cowed into submission.

'You don't really expect me to bear your children and then simply walk away when this sham marriage you fully expect to fail falls apart, do you?' she demanded, firming every sinew in her shocked body.

The faintest hint of something almost resembling compassion flashed across his face. Then it was gone so swiftly she wondered if she'd imagined it.

'Don't pretend it will be a hardship for you,' he said.

Anger at the cavalier way he dismissed her feelings bunched her fists. 'How can you say that? Of course it'll be a hardship for me! It'll be impossible. How dare you imply this is a decision to be taken lightly?'

His nostrils flared. 'We both know how flighty you can be. You say one thing and mean another. Do I need to remind you that I have first-hand knowledge of that? That you went straight from my arms into another man's with barely a pause in between? After you assured me that Paolo Romani meant nothing to you?'

The accusation stung, even though she knew the full truth behind it. The very real threats from her father...the vicious examples he'd made her witness. Her fear that he'd make true on them.

'Am I to bear punishment for one mistake for the rest of my life?'

The smile that curved his sensual lips was all cynicism, no mirth.

'But it wasn't just the one mistake, was it, *agape mou*? You knew I was there, listening, when you denigrated me to your father,' he accused, citing the awful night when they hadn't covered their tracks as well as they should have.

In her eagerness to meet with Ares in their secret spot, a few nights before her eighteenth birthday, she'd failed to ensure her father was otherwise occupied. Elio had found her in the orange grove. Her quick actions had thankfully ensured she seemed to be alone, but she'd been aware that Ares remained nearby, a protective presence but privy to every caustic put-down her father had unleashed upon her.

She'd remained silently defiant...until her father had whispered a vicious threat against Ares and Sergios. One so low and deadly she'd been certain Ares hadn't heard it.

Terror and panic had pushed her into responding regrettably, in the only way her young mind had offered.

She'd hotly denied her attraction to his chauffeur's son, and then gone one better and sworn he wasn't her type, that she'd never be attracted to him.

Even from his hidden spot, she'd felt the force of Ares's affront, the blow to his pride. And his cold rejection of her next day—the day she'd planned to go several steps further than the light kisses they'd so far shared—had hurt. Nevertheless, she'd understood.

She had hoped to explain that she'd said what she had to prevent the serious bodily harm her father had threatened Ares and his father with. She'd seen first-hand how Elio treated his enemies. The last thing she'd wanted was for him to act on his threats.

Until she'd discovered Ares's own plans.

*Ares Zanelis had always planned to leave her behind. To shatter the foolish, girlish dreams she'd woven around him.*

Having secured a string of near-dilapidated buildings with the nest egg his father had given him, he'd made plans to leave Alghero—information she'd discovered through the servants' gossip the day before he'd left.

Thankfully, he'd never witnessed the extent of her devastation. How she'd cried herself to sleep for months afterwards, with her father's cruel jabs at her clear unhappiness driving the knives in even deeper.

*Tell him now. Set the record straight.*

'I knew you were still in the orange grove that night, Ares. I said all those things to take my father's interest off you. I was protecting you. He threatened to have you beaten. Or worse.'

His mouth twisted, scoffing at the idea that a man like him would need someone to save him, even back then.

'Considerate of you. But I've never needed anyone to fight my battles for me. Bravo for trying—and you were shockingly convincing. Enough to make me wonder if it was your subconscious speaking the truth on your behalf.'

'No, it wasn't,' she protested hotly. 'I never thought you were beneath me.'

'You moved on very quickly after that. Or were you also protecting me when you kissed your father's lieutenant's son the very next night, in the same spot where you'd let me touch you?' he seethed.

Regret and shock ripped a gasp from her throat. 'You saw?'

Censure etched into his face. 'Oh, yes. But then I always saw you, didn't I? You made sure of that.'

'What do you mean by that?'

'It means we lived at opposite ends of your father's estate and had no business crossing paths—and yet there you always were.'

'You pursued me too!' she protested hotly, her face flaming.

He shrugged. 'You were as beautiful then as you are now. Perhaps as irresistible to me as you pretended I was to you. But you also proved to be fickle, didn't you? Maybe for once I shouldn't have ignored your father when he said you were meant for another. That I was a dress rehearsal for the real thing.'

She inhaled sharply. 'He said that to you?'

His sardonic smile widened. 'That and much more—including those threats you believed you were protecting me from. He never missed an opportunity to warn me away from the precious daughter he intended to marry off to Paolo Romani. The same bastard I saw you kissing, *agapita*,' he accused icily.

Odessa shook her head, choosing to remain silent. How could she tell him that it had been a misguided effort to forget him without sounding pathetic? That he'd been imprinted so deeply on her that she'd feared she would remain lonely for ever in the face of her father's determination to keep them apart? The formidable man beside her now would deem any excuse a weak protest, his judge-and-jury conviction of her character one she suspected he'd cemented a long time ago.

And more than his damning indictment it was the mocking endearment that threatened to flatten her. Because where it was all cynical now, he'd meant it once upon a time. Or had he? Had he, even back then, been skilfully adept at this level of hypnotic charm? Had she been so starved of care and affection that she'd seen only what he'd wanted her to see?

That cold wave of possibility made her stare harder, desperate to find the truth, or at the very least an inkling that she was wrong in her fears. She refused to be drawn back to the past. Not when this remarkable present demanded every atom of her concentration.

'I'll take your silence as an admission of guilt, shall I?' he asked.

She shook her head. 'No, it's not. I made a mistake. But whatever you think about me, I never misled you.'

Surprise flashed in his eyes, but again it was gone a nanosecond later.

This man's ability to master his emotions was almost fascinating to watch. *Almost.* Because Odessa would have given her eye teeth for a glimpse of lasting emotion. For some hope that the future he painted for her wasn't as terrifyingly bleak as it sounded. Not having his children. Oh, no. That had formed a big chunk of her teenage daydreams— the deep yearning to lovingly craft the antithesis of the family she'd been born into, *always* with Ares as the husband and father figure.

Hell, she'd foolishly confessed those dreams to him once, as they'd lazed under a lemon tree in one of those stolen summer nights when she'd sneaked out to meet him. That was why she wasn't surprised he wanted more than one child. He'd confessed that back then too, and they'd shared their antipathy to the loneliness of growing up without siblings. It was something they didn't wish on their children—

especially Ares, who'd known what it was like to have a sibling only to be robbed of her in the cruellest way possible.

God, had she supplied him with the very weapons to destroy her?

Sucking in a shaky breath, she opened her mouth to demand an answer to that horrifying possibility.

But he was exiting the car, his towering frame blotting out the light and throwing him into shadow as he came around, opened her door.

'Delving into our innermost feelings isn't why we're here. The clock is ticking, Odessa. What's it going to be?'

*One night.*

She'd insisted on one night to grapple with the most profound decision of her life, and already the hours were slipping through her fingers like wispy clouds burning in the sunlight.

Ares hadn't been happy with her unwavering demand. But she'd stood her ground, the stubborn defiance that had got her into trouble with her father more often than she cared to count asserting itself.

And holding firm had been bolstering. Perhaps even exhilarating.

Now, as she tossed and turned, the sheets twisting around her legs almost as tangled as her thoughts, her mind wasn't firm at all. Her thoughts veered from an outright *no* to his insane proposal to skirting the very edge of Ares's demands.

Could she...?

Her instinct shrieked a resounding *no*.

But the alternative...

She shivered at the thought of Ares throwing her back to the wolves. One wolf in particular—Vincenzo—who wouldn't hesitate to make her pay for the trick she'd pulled.

*She could run. Get up, grab her small case and just...run.*

And prove Ares correct in his denigration of her character? He already thought the worst of her. For unfathomable reasons, proving him right made her chest tighten unbearably.

She'd given her word.

And, yes, she'd landed herself in this situation with that *'I'll do anything'* she'd stupidly blurted out.

Because she'd never thought he'd ask her for *this*!

But the alternative…

The shiver that gripped her now was colder, more ominous in a way that she couldn't overlook. Going back to Alghero would be akin to a death sentence, with her uncle choosing to look the other way despite being fully aware of Vincenzo's intended treatment of her. The alternative—walking away from Ares and striking out on her own—would mean her looking over her shoulder for the rest of her life. Maybe even worse. Because no amount of defiance would keep her safe from Uncle Flávio or Vincenzo. And once she was caught, Vincenzo, like all men of his ilk, would force her to breed, just to prove his manhood.

Wouldn't she be better off staying here? Bearing Ares's children?

The very idea that she was even considering it made her squeeze her eyes shut, smashing her face into the pillow until the scream trapped in her throat ripped free.

The picture that formed in the aftermath of that tiny catharsis didn't repulse her, like thoughts of Vincenzo did. Hell, it was the opposite. She'd dreamed of bearing Ares's children once upon a time.

But that had been the daydream of a forcibly sheltered girl on the cusp of womanhood, whose only true exposure to the opposite sex had been the tall, dark Greek with brooding, hungry eyes. Hadn't it?

She exhaled, her eyes flying open, in a wild bid to dispel the thoughts weaving so seductively in her head. The whispered *what ifs* that pressed so heavily on her, demanding attention. Ares's terms said five years, after which they would separate...*if* she wanted to leave. That meant the option to stay was hers. Wasn't it?

What if she agreed to his terms—for now—with a view to altering them later?

Odessa gulped down a rising bolt of unease. But it wouldn't diminish.

She'd requested his help on a wild whim that had saved her from a fate worse than death. Dared she risk gambling again, on making this work too?

Her thoughts were still spinning when she finally fell into a restless sleep.

Alarmingly she felt stronger when she woke, showered and dressed a few short hours later, and then went to find the man who'd put his ring on her finger last night, and tossed her world into pure chaos.

The sun was barely peeking through the ancient Roman buildings, but Ares was already up and dressed, sipping an espresso on the same terrace Odessa had used yesterday.

He rose from the pristinely set table the moment she stepped out, dressed once more in her jeans and another simple top, and she couldn't fail to see the contrast between them.

But for all his suave exterior and iron composure, his neatly combed hair and polished shoes, there was a coiled tension within him, an intensity in his eyes, that said her answer mattered to him. That perhaps he'd donned this bespoke armour because there was a chink he was determined to guard.

Delusional, perhaps, but Odessa ruthlessly clung to that, the same way she'd excavated pockets of defiance to fight her oppression over the years. She'd lost more than she'd won, but fighting had kept her spirits alive. And as long as she had breath in her body she'd keep fighting.

Especially if she was fighting for her children.

Because somewhere in the early hours she'd reasoned that if Ares truly was doing this for his father, and he wasn't completely heartless in his endeavour, then perhaps at some point down the road she might sway him into accepting a different, better role than full custody.

*And if he didn't?*

She shrugged inwardly. Then she'd just fight harder.

She'd persuaded him into granting her a lifeline out of the hell she'd faced in her father's house, hadn't she?

'Odessa.'

Her name was a command. And, really, wasn't she just torturing herself by withholding the answer she'd decided to give?

Slicking her tongue over dry lips, she stepped forward. The vital need to look into his eyes and see something… anything that would give her hope…was too compelling to deny.

'It's a yes, Ares. My answer is yes.'

She saw it then. The quiet exhalation. The release of tension. The flash of relief in his eyes.

She held up her hand when he opened his mouth to speak.

'But before you celebrate, you should know this. I won't abandon my children. *Ever.* No matter what.'

His eyes glinted fiercely with layers of triumph, then surprise, before settling on heavy scepticism. 'We'll just have to wait and see, won't we?'

He might deny them, but she intended to remind herself of those vital tells. Frequently.

Ares wasn't inhuman.

She *would* change his mind down the road.

Anything else was unthinkable.

She raised her chin, met his gaze. 'Hold your breath if you want. Or don't. I won't even bother with *I told you so* when the time comes.'

They landed in Athens later that afternoon to frenzied tabloid interest.

One of their own—powerful and influential, the shining epitome of rags to riches—had snagged himself a beautiful bride. A woman he'd apparently grown up with, they breathlessly reported. Perhaps even a childhood sweetheart?

Ares held her hand, kissed her knuckles and brushed his lips over her temple. His eyes locked hungrily on hers. And he ignored the shouted questions.

Beside them, Sergios beamed, his approval clear despite the sometimes circumspect looks he levelled at Odessa.

For her part, she kept her mouth shut, for fear she'd blurt something untoward or reveal that, contrary to the paparazzi's view, it wasn't a fairy tale marriage. Hell, they hadn't even discussed when or where they'd be getting married.

'First things first,' Ares drawled when they were ensconced in another sleek limo, his fingers flying over his phone screen.

'What?'

'You need a new wardrobe. Would you prefer to go shopping or shall I have a selection brought to you?'

She frowned. 'I don't need new clothes.'

'You intend to wear those jeans on every occasion until they fall off you?'

She opened her mouth to argue, then pursed them again when she accepted that he had a point. 'Fine, but I can buy my own clothes.'

As Ares Zanelis' wife, and soon-to-be mother of his children, she clearly had an image to project. The full scope of his existence had only just come into focus for her in the last day.

There would be no enforced seclusion on a cliff-front estate the way her father had hidden her away. The thought was at once freeing and mildly panic-inducing.

The hand that reached for hers and patted it gently was surprisingly not Ares's. She glanced up at Sergios's benign smile.

'My son can be overbearing at times. He can't help himself. But you deserve to be spoilt, *mikros*. And besides, all women enjoy shopping, *ne*?' Leaning forward, he stage-whispered, 'Or you can get your own back by dragging him along with you while you spend his money. I'm told it's a fate worse than death.'

Aware of Ares's sharp gaze—and with the reminder that they were pretending at the very least to be wildly attracted to each other with a view to starting a family—she summoned a smile in return. Then her gaze caught on the landscape whizzing by, in the very first country she'd ever visited outside Italy.

'I'll choose my clothes, thanks,' she answered.

'*Kalos*. I've cleared my calendar for the afternoon,' Ares said.

Surprise widened her eyes. 'You have?'

'*Ne*. And while we're out we can discuss wedding plans.'

That combination of panic and excitement fizzled harder. 'Already?'

His eyes gleamed, sweeping over her face in a blatant appraisal that made heat pummel her. 'I don't see any point in waiting. I want us to start our lives together. Don't you?'

The pointed question was a veiled reminder of their agreement.

Exhaling for composure, she replied, 'Yes, I do.'

Satisfaction darkened the gleam.

Across from her, Sergios's smile widened.

Her heart thumping wildly in her chest, Odessa gazed out of the window, where the vibrant streets of Athens impressed upon her the fact that her life was well on course to change irreparably.

Ares finished the next call on his list, tuning out the sales assistants' excited chattering as they flitted around Odessa. He sat in the waiting room of a luxury boutique, an untouched glass of Dom Perignon ignored at his elbow, as he continued to make plans as if the devil himself were snapping at his heels.

His father had been right. This was torture. But not in the way Sergios had meant. It was torture because Ares couldn't seem to find the willpower to get up and walk out. Leave Odessa to her own devices.

He'd thought he'd be satisfied once she'd agreed to his demands. Instead, that peculiar sense of urgency had only escalated. He wasn't sure whether it was a good or a bad trait he possessed that meant once he set his mind to a thing he tended not to rest until his goal was achieved.

Pausing on his next phone call, he examined his true feelings for a minute, in the wild hope that it would clear his mind of this idiotic urgency.

Even now he could hear the assistants cooing over the engagement ring he'd procured yesterday with that same driving agitation.

Was it the five years already ticking down? Was he so eager for this project to be underway? So he could see if he was dealing with the same kind of situation his mother had put him through? Or was it more that since Odessa's vehement protests in the car last night he'd yearned for a crystal ball, to see whether she would stay true to her word? If she would deliver on some of the foolish, forgotten promises she'd eagerly made all those years ago.

And wasn't that a hell of a thing to crave? Especially when he knew better...

And...*mummy issues*? Really?

He wanted to scoff at the thought, but he couldn't deny that it was there, a glaring black hole in his life he'd never been able to distance himself from.

While he was sure some therapists would lay the blame of his reluctance to marry on his tragic situation, Ares knew it was a series of events, ending with the woman currently hidden behind heavy curtains, trying on the clothes he intended to grace her stunning body with, who'd cemented his decision never to encumber himself with a wife.

Or at least he'd believed that until her impassioned protest that she'd been attempting to *save* him. To place herself between him and her vicious father.

Ares shifted in his seat, the recollection dragging an unfamiliar uncertainty from him. But even if she'd meant that, he couldn't ignore her other actions. How swiftly she'd turned away from him and into another man's arms.

His mother's desertion and cruelty had taught him that he didn't need a wife or a so-called life partner to enhance his life. Hell, the lack of one would remove any threat of rejection altogether for his future offspring. Better to start off with zero expectations than harbour foolish notions, right?

*Ne.*

Control reasserted, he straightened as Odessa stepped out. 'Leave us, please.'

The assistants scurried away immediately, but it took him another handful of seconds to drag his gaze from her stunning body and the control-wrecking things the black lace dress did to her figure.

He pulled up the images on his phone and turned the

screen to her, watching closely as she swiped through the pictures, her breath catching as she glanced up.

'It's breathtaking. Where is that?'

'Ismene—my private island. We'll get married there a week from today. Does that work for you?'

He expected her to protest, or the very least make a show of unhappiness. To his surprise, she handed his phone back and shrugged.

'Sure, why not. It's not like I have any pressing engagements. It looks like a perfect place for a wedding.' She looked over her shoulder. 'Is there something else you want to discuss, or shall I get the assistants back?'

His fingers drummed restlessly on his thighs. 'No, that's all.'

She turned immediately, dismissing his presence. He bit back a growl.

'Odessa?'

She paused, silver eyes flicking to his. *'Si?'*

He nudged his chin at the black lace dress. 'Keep that dress. I like it.'

Satisfaction at her blush was short-lived. And for the life of him Ares couldn't understand why his grouchy mood persisted as the hours passed.

Perhaps it was because, unlike women he'd known in the past, she didn't gush with joy at being lavished with hundreds of thousands of euros' worth of clothes and jewels. Or because she mostly ignored him, chatting happily to Sergios during dinner and at breakfast the next morning.

He'd saved her, damn it—in a twisted knight in shining armour situation he was almost convinced had been orchestrated by his father.

Where was her gratitude? Her hero-worship?

Hell, she'd been insultingly eager when she'd excused herself to meet with the wedding co-ordinator he'd lined up to visit before they left for Ismene. And she was equally perky on the way back home now, her interest in the local landmarks reminding him of how cloistered she'd been in Alghero.

Ares stopped himself from playing the tour guide—from postponing their imminent departure to Ismene so he could take her on an extended tour of his beloved Athens.

She wasn't here on a sightseeing trip.

She was here to take his name, to bear his children, and then to be monitored with eagle eyes if she so much as hinted at taking a leaf out of his mother's book.

*'Hold your breath if you want to. Or don't...'*

Challenging words. But she didn't know him well if she thought he wouldn't accept that gauntlet.

He would be right there when she failed. And this time if she betrayed him he'd dispatch Odessa Santella and there would be no going back.

Goals reaffirmed, he grabbed his tablet, ignoring the woman whose head was now whipping back and forth, who gasped delightfully at her first sight of the Acropolis, her neck craned with almost endearing eagerness until the iconic landmark was out of view.

# CHAPTER FIVE

CONTRARY TO HER belief that the week would speed towards the moment she married Ares, Odessa thought it crawled by treacle-slowly. So slowly so that she came within a whisper of suggesting they bring the date forward.

She only held her tongue because, despite her bravado, nerves were killing her.

Also because her feigned flippancy seemed to get under Ares's skin, and for some insane reason she preferred his brooding watchfulness and rasped interrogation about every aspect of her wedding planning to his icy aloofness.

It had started when he'd shown her the breathtaking private island where they were to wed. The punch of pure joy on seeing the setting, plucked straight from every daydream she'd ever harboured about her wedding day, had disturbed her enough to scramble to hide it, inadvertently sparking a restive reaction in him. Almost as if he needed regular evidence that she meant to keep her word.

She'd made a game of providing it, having no qualms about interrupting his work day to ask his opinion about linen colour themes or primary flower choices.

It was a situation Sergios had found hilarious, egging her on with winks and approving nods.

Their one serious clash had come when she'd protested that she didn't want anything from him when their marriage ended. That had drawn a sceptical glare that had sent his lawyers scrambling away to give them privacy. And in the ensuing twenty minutes she'd discovered just how cynical this new, mega-successful Ares had become.

No, he *didn't* believe her pious claim not to want anything from him.

No, he *wasn't* about to accept that she wouldn't sue him for a stake of his fortune further down the line.

Yes, her protests were useless.

To shut him up, Odessa had signed the prenup that granted her twenty million euros should they divorce. A fortune most people would give their eye-teeth for, but to her would mean she was leaving something vital behind.

They'd carried on like that until now, the morning before the wedding, when a less formally dressed but still furnace-hot Ares entered the living room where she was watching TV with Sergios after breakfast—although the old man had already dozed off in his favourite chair.

'Are you ready?' he drawled, his gaze shifting over her in that mildly possessive way he'd taken to using when looking at her, then returning to her face and her puzzled frown. 'Did you check your phone?'

She grabbed the sleek new phone he'd handed her the morning after their arrival. There, tucked away in a text box, was his prompt about a ten a.m. appointment.

'Where are we going? Do I need to change?'

His gaze slid down her floral wraparound dress to the matching wedge heels. 'You're fine as you are. We're going to see my private doctor.'

'I'm to be checked over to see if I fit my brood mare status, am I?' she blurted before she could stop herself.

The time she'd had to dwell on what was happening was taking its toll on her nerves.

He slanted her an enigmatic look. 'The examination isn't for just you. It's for both of us.'

Surprise snatched her breath away. 'You're getting checked too?'

'Indeed. If only to make sure my robust stallion status is at premium level.'

It took her a startling moment to realise he was cracking a joke. Her lips curved in response, her heart leaping. For a second while Ares had forgotten himself she'd caught a glimmer of the younger man she remembered.

Even after his amusement waned, she let that memory sustain her. Let it shore her up to withstand this older version's more dynamic battering of her senses.

That glimmer made another fleeting appearance when they were both pronounced rudely healthy two hours later, and a layer of tension left his shoulders.

In contrast, her own heartbeat escalated when she noticed that his gaze had grown even more brooding, the hand he placed on her back as they left his doctor's office that much more possessive. Even in the car and heading home he kept her close, his eyes pinned on her in a way that made her hackles rise.

'You're acting strangely. Is something wrong?'

He cupped her jaw in his strong hand, his hold making her feel far too delicate, its gentleness opening those vulnerable spaces within her she needed to keep shut.

'Not at all. I'm appreciating the fact that nothing stands in our way now. You're mine. There's no getting away from me now, *glykia mou*.'

The raw, primitive throb of possessiveness should have alarmed her. And yet, unlike every dark omen visited upon her in the past, Ares's words made her heart race with fevered yearning.

No matter the circumstances that had triggered this, the

end result would be special and life-changing. A secret yearning brought to life.

*If the trend of her cycle went according to plan, she could be pregnant by this time next month.*

'There's one thing we need to discuss.' She cursed the heat rushing into her face, but the subject was too important to ignore. 'How I'm going to get pregnant. I'm assuming it'll be through IVF—'

The wicked and humourless laugh dried her words. 'No, *agapita*. You assume wrong. When I said everything about this marriage would be real, I meant it. And *everything* includes your presence in my bed every night until we are absolutely certain my seed is growing in your womb. Even then, I reserve the right to perform my marital duties.'

She gaped at him, askance, while the feverish cyclone inside her swirled higher. 'But…why? You don't even want me that way.'

His eyes narrowed. 'And how did you come to that conclusion?'

'Come off it, Ares. At this point I'm fairly sure you don't even like me!'

A muscle ticked at his temple. 'Do I need to like you to put a baby in your belly?' he asked.

But the query wasn't as clinical as the words suggested. And beneath the steady, almost mocking regard, she sensed he wasn't quite as calm as he projected.

It was almost admirable—to a point.

'How did I not see this crafty version of you back then?' she murmured.

His mouth twisted and his thumb drifted almost absent-mindedly over her cheek. 'Perhaps you preferred to see your own version of the truth. I have always been like this.'

Her fists bunched. She refused to accept that she'd been so hoodwinked. 'I don't believe that I could've been so blind.'

'Then that's on you, Odessa.'

They stared each other down for an age, then she sucked in a breath. 'Then maybe I should be thankful things turned out the way they did.'

His face shuttered completely, and he withdrew his touch a moment later. 'Indeed. But it doesn't change the fact that you'll come to me on our wedding night and I will possess you completely.'

Ismene was halfway between Athens and Crete, east of Santorini. The four-square-kilometre jewel in the South Aegean was the stuff of fairy tales and endless opulence, with its reality far surpassing what the pictures had promised.

As they circled the island in preparation to land, Odessa spotted the beginnings of a marquee and a flower-festooned arched trellis on one pristine lawn a short distance from a white sandy beach, and that punch of illicit excitement returned.

'If I had my way we'd be married before sundown tonight,' Ares murmured beside her, making her jolt as his breath washed over her ear. 'But my father insists I must not be a complete brute about the entire thing, so you'll get to find your bearings, rest and enjoy your last night as a free woman.'

He caught her hand in his and raised it to his lips.

Her stomach dipped with the altitude of the landing plane, and a thrill lanced her, despite knowing he was putting on a show for Sergios, who watched them with another indulgent smile.

The villa was a single-storey sprawling gem, with more inviting outdoor terraces than she could count, all of them showcasing a breath-catching view and an open invitation to bask in the gorgeous Greek sun.

The staff of six, headed by a buxom grey-haired matriarch in her sixties, greeted her with halting Italian and Ares and Sergios with lyrical Greek, their beckoning leading them to a large table laid out with refreshments.

Whether intended or not, the table overlooked the part of the garden being decorated for the wedding.

'Interested in seeing all your hard work up close?' Ares asked, his gaze intent on her face as he handed her a sparkling drink.

The force with which she wanted to say *yes* almost sucked the breath from her. It was that rabid yearning that made her hesitate. She couldn't afford for her feelings to become embroiled in this.

'It's your wedding. Some would say it's your absolute right to interfere,' he said.

'The organiser has been very accommodating, but I think I'm this close to earning myself a Bridezilla label,' she murmured.

Sergios slid her a plate of sugar-coated snacks. 'Nonsense. You have a kind heart, *mikros*. That is what I've always liked about you. But Ares is right. You have a right to see to it that your special day is exactly as you want, *ne*?'

She smiled at him, his words warming her as always. 'Okay,' she replied, and then her heart thudded harder as they both rose with her.

Together they approached the lawn where the stunning wedding arch had been constructed, the white and purple flowers she'd settled on expertly woven into the trellis. She'd known the end result would be any bride's dream. And even if she wasn't *the* dreamy bride, she couldn't stop her heart fluttering at the knowledge that she was about to marry Ares Zanelis, the man of her deepest fantasies.

After which she'd be just a brood mare, forced to accept the trappings of marriage so Ares could ensure his bloodline and please his father.

'It all looks perfect,' she said, despite the vice tightening in her chest. She tagged on a smile for Sergios's sake. Ares, she ignored, not risking a glance his way in case he caught her anguish.

Forcing herself to eat a few bites of the refreshments, she allowed the conversation between the two men to wash over her.

The reappearance of the housekeeper brought a hidden sigh of relief.

'Demeter will show you to our suite,' Ares told her. 'We'll have dinner early tonight.'

Her eyes widened at the *'our'*, but she couldn't ask the question bubbling on her tongue. His pointed look answered her anyway. They would be sharing sleeping space for the foreseeable future. At the very least until he'd planted his seed in her womb.

She turned away, hoping he didn't see her flush at the thought.

It turned out she needn't have been so disturbed by the prospect of sharing a bed with Ares. The suite was vast, and as she followed Demeter into the sprawling space she realised there were *two* bedrooms, linked by a sumptuous private living area, a wraparound terrace and even a plunge pool that could easily accommodate a dozen people.

It was easy enough to identify Ares's domain from the bold slate-grey and white colour scheme. And as Demeter showed her to where her things had been unpacked and neatly placed in the white and soft lilac themed dressing room that matched the second bedroom, she told herself that the hollow feeling in her belly had nothing to with the anti-climax of realising she wouldn't be sharing a bed with Ares immediately.

That it was merely relief...

*  *  *

Starting as she meant to carry on, Odessa latched on to one excuse after another for the next twelve hours.

When Ares didn't show up for dinner, a twinkly-eyed Sergios eagerly cited the fact that his son had decided to honour the tradition of not seeing his bride the night before the wedding.

Then, in the morning, she excused the butterflies in her belly as indigestion rather than pre-wedding jitters.

Even the tears that filled her eyes when the wedding couturier inserted the last diamond hairpin into the elaborate up-do, set the stylish veil on her head and finally allowed Odessa to catch the first glimpse of herself in her bridal gown, she excused as over-tiredness and the fraught situation.

*Not* the fact that the dress was plucked straight out of her dreams and had made her heart leap the first time she'd spotted it, its halter-neck silk overlaid with delicate lace that cinched in at the waist, moulded her hips and flared slightly at the knees to end in a short train.

*Not* the fact that underneath it she wore her mother's locket and couldn't help but yearn for her presence today.

And most definitely *not* the fact that the man whose name she would be taking an hour from now continued to be the only man her conscious and subconscious continued to conjure up every time she dared to dwell on who her ideal husband and the father of her children would be.

All that denial threatened to bubble over and explode when, finally ready, she stepped out of the suite and found Sergios waiting, looking nervous and hopeful and so endearing in his tuxedo, with a rosette of the same tiny flowers that were woven into her bouquet and hair inserted into his lapel.

His gaze swept over her, and Odessa was almost certain he blinked back tears.

Before she could speak, he grasped her hands. 'I know this isn't tradition, but it would be my honour to escort you down the aisle—if you'll let me?'

Odessa swallowed a lump in her throat. 'Are...are you sure?'

He squeezed her fingers, his voice gruff as he said, '*Ne, mikros*. Very much.'

Pressing her lips together to stop emotion bubbling free, and wishing her own father had taken a single leaf out of this man's book when he'd been alive, she smiled shakily. 'Thank you.'

That shakiness continued as they went down the stairs to the hall, to be flanked by smiling household staff, organisers and wait-staff, who murmured genial wishes, and then outside to join the small but impressive gathering of people she didn't know, invited by Ares to witness his marriage.

Then every scrap of her attention was captured by the man who stood beneath the immaculate arch, his complete focus riveted on her, with not a single sign of the nerves eating her alive on his face.

He wore a bespoke slate grey suit, its lines falling on his form with mouth-watering perfection.

His gaze flicked to his father for a nanosecond, a potent look passing between them before those eyes returned to her. Locked.

It was almost as if she was all he could see. All he wanted to see.

Under other fantastical circumstances Odessa might have allowed herself to be swept away into sheer bliss by that look. But she knew what it meant. It was a look of pure conquest. She'd handed herself over on a platter and he intended to devour every last piece of her.

When they finally reached the top of the aisle, father and son exchanged another long, speaking look, which was topped off with an approving nod from Sergios.

Then Ares was facing her, grasping the hands his father had just released, raising the one bearing his dazzling engagement ring to his lips.

The resulting electricity only added to the fireworks occurring within her, and again Odessa had to caution herself that it was all for show—the same as when he raked her with a heated gaze and murmured throatily, 'You look exquisite, *eros mou*,' in a way that made the priest smile and nod, thoroughly ignorant and approving the compliment.

She tried not to let those fanciful fireworks consume her as they repeated the vows that would bind them together. She scrambled for pragmatism when afterwards they walked back down the white-carpeted aisle and into the marquee overlooking the ocean where their reception was to be held. It was decorated with lavish ice sculptures, and priceless caviar and vintage champagne flowed.

And she clawed that pragmatism especially close when Ares took her in his arms, possessiveness blazing in his eyes and running through the body that he pulled dizzyingly tight against her as they swayed in their first dance.

'Once again I find myself wishing time and everyone away,' he murmured in her ear, and the twist of his mouth in an attempt at humour was immediately eroded by the heated purpose in his eyes.

'Because you want this to be over as quickly as possible?' she ventured, even while the see-sawing in her belly made a mockery of that flippant response.

The heat intensified. 'On the contrary... When we're finally alone I'll wish for time to stand still, so I can savour the moment.'

The thick layers of anticipation and exultation were hard

to dismiss when they ruffled her own unsettled emotions so expertly.

'Gloating is a sin,' she told him. 'You know that, right?'

His flawless teeth flashed in unabashed elation as he pressed her closer still, his breath brushing her cheek as he said, 'I welcome the punishment. Because nothing and no one will stop me from savouring every inch of you, *matia mou*. As much as I have wished to deny it, I can't help but accept that I've waited a long time for this moment. And make no mistake: I mean to take it.'

There was nothing to say to that, even if she'd managed to speak above the traitorous currents rushing through her while she battled for her heart to remain above this erotic and emotional fray.

The battle continued as Ares handed her over to his father for the next dance, and as they were toasted and showered with gifts from well-wishers. And then, once Ares had draped a flawless diamond bracelet on her wrist, and drawn the requisite gasps from their guests, he was swinging her into his arms and striding off with her to raucous applause.

He didn't stop until he'd crossed the threshold into his… *their*…suite.

When she glanced longingly at her side of the room, he intercepted the look and shook his head. 'Oh, no. You won't be returning there for quite some time,' he rasped in her ear.

Her foundations had grown shaky, but she still fought on. 'Can we talk about this?'

'No. The time for talking is over. Accept it. Unless you mean to go back on your word?' he dared, his eyes blazing into hers.

Hating him a little, for knowing the exact buttons to push, she raised her chin. 'Never.'

The slightest tinge of relief in his eyes was wiped away by triumph as he strode up to the bed, then slid her down to her feet. She couldn't fail to notice the hard, screamingly male angles of his body, or easily dismiss their effect on her.

Nor could she fail to take in how imposing his king-sized bed was up close. She'd only looked at it briefly when Demeter had escorted her to her room yesterday. Now, the waist-high mattress festooned with pillows and sleek sheets evoked images that sent pulses of fire though her veins, burning her from the inside out.

But while she was dying with nerves at the thought of the unknown—because she'd only done this once before, in a furtive, shamefully unremarkable three-minute fumble that had left her mourning the gift she'd so carelessly thrown away—Ares was simply…watching her.

As if now he had her he wanted to stretch out the inevitable.

Well, she didn't.

In a blind need to stop the rollercoaster, she reached for the diamond bracelet he'd gifted her just an hour ago.

His hand flashed out, stopped her. 'No. Leave that on. In fact…'

He caught her wrist and tugged her after him towards a painting she suspected would more than hold its own at the Uffizi.

'What are you doing?' she asked, when he pressed a hidden button and the painting sprang a couple of inches away from the wall.

Behind it she saw a state-of-the-art safe, inserted into the wall. With a thumbprint and a swiftly entered code, the thick door popped open. Ares released her long enough to pull out two pouches and a large oblong box that screamed more priceless jewellery.

She was proved right when, after sliding his hand around her waist and nudging her to the bed, he upended the contents of all three, leaving her wide eyed, mouth agape.

'Indulging another fantasy. What else?' he answered her belatedly.

'A fantasy?' she echoed, part of her not wanting to know what that might have been because it would make what was happening so much more unbearable.

His gaze turned a touch heavy, almost contemplative. 'I left Alghero with little above a pittance in my pocket, but with big ambitions and perhaps foolish dreams.' He shrugged. 'One of those was to drape you in diamonds at the very first opportunity,' he rasped.

Pain stung her heart. 'But you left without telling me—'

He pressed his fingers to her lips and his jaw clenched a touch before he released it.

'I don't wish to start this with disharmony. Turn around,' he instructed.

She complied—partly because she wanted a reprieve from the intensity in his eyes. But the touch of his fingers at her nape, brushing her bare skin as he freed the silk-covered buttons one by one, was torture in itself.

The dress pooled at her feet, leaving her clad in only a pair of white lace panties that barely covered the lower half of her butt cheeks.

Ares inhaled sharply and she felt the agitated rise and fall of his chest, felt her skin burning with the ferocity of his regard.

'*Thee mou.* You are Aphrodite herself,' he breathed, a moment before firm hands gripped her waist and tugged her back against the hot pillar of his body.

It was her turn to lose her breath. The sensation of being plastered against him was so searing, and so divine, a moan escaped before she could stop herself.

He caressed her waist for several seconds, then leaned past her and plucked the first gem set off the bed. The cold touch of a platinum chain puckered her nipples and beaded her skin. She glanced down, her eyes widening at the sight of a diamond-studded body chain, at the centre of which hung a shorter pendant chain that ended in a thumb-sized teardrop diamond.

She was so busy being awestruck at this very personal, very erotic piece of jewellery, she didn't notice her panties were halfway down her thighs until Ares lifted her free of them.

Blushing, she drew her hands up to shield herself.

He caught her wrists and firmly drew them away, then turned her around. 'No, *yineka mou*. Your breathtaking body was made to wear priceless diamonds,' he muttered thickly, and then his gaze roved her body, his breathing turning harsher as he took in her naked diamond-ornamented form. 'You are even better than I dreamt you'd be.'

Before she could even begin to grasp the fact that he'd dreamed of this, he was continuing, almost to himself.

'Perhaps I should commission more of these...'

'Please don't.'

His head reared up, eyebrows rising. 'Why not? Most women would—'

She snatched her hands from his, blind and hot jealousy punching her in the chest. 'I'm not "most women". I think the earlier we establish that, the better it will be for both of us.'

He leaned forward, brushed the tip of her nose with his, then inhaled deeply. For whatever reason, the move immediately calmed her roiling emotions.

'*Ne*, you're right. You're my wife. And as such you hold a special place.'

Somewhat mollified, she bit her tongue against further protests. She'd learned a long time ago that an intransigent Ares was as immovable as Vesuvius.

'I will have one made for here...' He trailed the fingers of both hands over her clavicle, then down between her breasts to the upper curve of her waist. 'And then another to pay homage to this glorious piece of heaven.'

His arms circled under her waist to her bottom, grabbing both globes in his hands before he let loose a deep, throaty groan.

'Ares...'

'I'm in two minds about how to decorate these, though...'

He dipped his head, flicked his tongue over one nipple, then sealed his hot mouth over it. Heated arrows shot between her legs, stinging and dampening her core with such sweet pleasure she cried out, her hands darting up to grab his shoulders before her weakened knees gave way.

'*Dio*...please.' A full-body tremor shook through her.

'Please what, *matia mou*?' he muttered, his tongue still shamelessly lapping at her painfully aroused buds.

She convulsed, her nails digging into him. 'You...you don't need to torture me. You already have what you want.'

'And what's that?' he asked, with a hint of tightness in his tone.

'Me. You have me. Can't that be enough?'

He straightened, replaced his mouth with his hands, and moulded her breasts as he took his time to consider that.

'No. Not until my seed is fully implanted and growing in your womb. Then I may consider this thing halfway to being successful.'

With that, he nudged her firmly backwards, watched her tumble onto the bed with triumph blazing in his eyes. Then he was prowling over her, dragging her up until she lay there, displayed like the sacrifice he fully meant her to be, in the middle of his bed.

He reared back then, settling on his knees and tugging off his jacket. He watched her with fixated intensity. Tossing it away, he undid several shirt buttons, then ditched his undressing and grabbed the next piece of jewellery.

An anklet.

Shamefully aroused, Odessa watched him tug one of her legs up. One large hand circled her ankle, brought her leg up to rest her foot against his bare chest, while the other trailed the delicate anklet which bore the same yellow teardrop diamond as its centrepiece up her inner thigh.

Shivers racked her body, drawing a wicked smile to his arousal-etched face. 'You're so intoxicatingly responsive...' he rasped thickly.

After securing the piece, he raised her foot, dropped a kiss on her instep, then slowly widened her legs until her core was bare to his rabid gaze.

Until he couldn't miss how wet, how thoroughly turned on she was.

'I've waited a long time for this,' he breathed. There was a heavy vein of satisfaction in his voice, but also a sliver of bittersweetness to his confession.

'You don't sound happy about it.'

'As much as the end result is satisfactory, if I'd had my way it would've happened much sooner.'

Her heart lurched. She opened her mouth—to say what, exactly, she wasn't sure. It wasn't to apologise again. At this point Odessa deemed she'd served whatever penance she deserved for her actions on her eighteenth birthday.

As much as it hurt, the ball was in Ares's court.

His thumb slid a little roughly, insistent, over her mouth from top to bottom, then along her lower lip. His breathing intensified as she parted her lips, her body surging into stinging life as he explored her with the avidity of pirates exploring their loot.

For the longest time they simply existed in that thickened bubble of sensate touch, their breaths mingling as arousal mounted.

'Suck,' he ordered gruffly, sliding his thumb tightly between her lips.

She closed her lips immediately, her nipples peaking and a soft moan floating up from her throat at the dirty, sublime sensation.

'*Theos...*' he cursed, voice hoarse, eyes so dark they were almost black.

Odessa's face flamed as triumph blazed in his eyes, unable to look away as he undid his belt and tugged down his zipper. Then—again as if he couldn't help himself—he abandoned his undressing and trailed his fingers down her body from throat to midriff, to circle her belly button before slowing his caress to pause where the diamond lay against her mound. His eyes rising to lock on hers, he slipped his fingers lower, lower, until his hand completely covered her femininity.

'Mine.'

Primal. Raw. *Absolute.*

Her every nerve-ending shuddered at this visceral possessiveness.

'Say it,' he insisted.

'Y-yours,' she whispered, drowning in sensation.

Sliding his thumb out of her mouth, he dropped forward and then onto one elbow, hazel eyes still locked on hers, his fingers between her thighs.

He caressed her while slowly plucking the pins out of her hair. The diamond fasteners scattered onto the bed, each one glinting and sparkling as her restless body moved under his expert ministrations. And even as he took his time to spread her hair all over his pillow, whispering sensual Greek words in her ear, the fingers between her thighs moved faster, strumming that nerve-filled nub and driving her to the pinnacle of insanity.

Odessa's cries grew louder as sensation built and built and *built*. As the tension gripping her body reached feverpitch and she had no choice but to dig her fingers into his thick biceps, to hold on as heady and terrifying bliss rushed at her.

'Ne...' he encouraged, his fingers spearing into her hair to hold her still, to direct her gaze to his, before he commanded huskily, 'Give it up, Odessa. Come for me. *Now.*'

Pleasure annihilated her, and it was made more electrifying by his rapt absorption in her every reaction, the way he hungrily devoured her surrender, then fused his lips to hers as her climax abated.

Her breathing was still worryingly agitated when she felt him rise, his fingers leaving her. It made her want to protest. But she knew he wasn't done with her. And that mortifying need for more turned her head, let her watch him as he finally shook off his remaining clothes.

Ares in his early twenties had been breathtaking. A decade later, with time and intelligence and maturity thrown into the mix, his raw masculinity was utterly enthralling.

'You like what you see?' he asked, his hands braced on his hips, positively entrenched in his confidence and unabashed about his impressive erection.

Heat suffused her face, drawing low, deep laughter from him as she dragged her gaze away.

'It's okay...you don't need to answer. I can tell for myself.'

Her eyes flew to his and he held them for a moment before staring blatantly at her peaked nipples and her twisting thighs. As much as she wanted to deny her body's reaction, it was no use. He knew how overwhelmingly he affected her. What was the point in hiding it?

She forced herself to relax her limbs, felt her own confidence growing when she saw her effect on him. It was a good time to be reminded that back then he'd seemed captivated by her. Not as much as she'd been by him, but enough for her to accept that perhaps, all these years later, this thing wasn't one-sided.

After all, would he still be so incensed about that kiss on her eighteenth birthday if he didn't care?

Buoyed by the reminder, she raised her hands and raked her fingers through her hair, pushing it away from her sweat-sheened skin.

Fierce dark eyes followed the movement, and then she watched him swallow. Watched him jerk forward onto the bed, as if compelled by a power beyond him, to resume his position between her thighs.

Her confidence threatened to falter then. Because he was big. Overwhelming. Once again she was so focused on him that he was all she could see. All she could *feel*.

And when he took her mouth in a bold kiss, he was all she could taste.

The kiss was decadent. Control-wrecking.

The slide of his hand down the same path it had taken a handful of minutes ago reignited barely banked flames. Higher. More ferocious.

His hair-roughened thighs parted her smooth ones…

And there, among the priceless diamonds, the greedy grasping and sliding of flesh, the devilishly sublime feasting and quickly snatched breaths, Ares Zanelis finally possessed the forbidden princess he'd coveted for far too long and against all logical reasoning.

He basked in her smooth, silkiness. Exulted in her hitched breath as he entered her for the first time and her sublime, warm, *tight* sheath momentarily addled his brain before a deep breath restored a fraction of his mental prowess.

It was enough for him to luxuriate in her hungry cries, her broken demands for *more* and then for mercy. To watch her glorious mane ripple on his sheets in the way he'd yearned to see for so long. To watch his diamonds glitter on her skin the way he'd vowed they would an aeon ago, battling for supremacy against her sublime beauty and failing to outshine Odessa Santella...

*No, Odessa Zanelis.*

And even in this, Ares smugly concluded, his name sounded better alongside hers.

*Wherever you are in hell, old man, I hope this makes you burn faster.*

He drove harder into her, roared when she screamed his name and clung to him as if he were the last raft in a world-ending tempest. Then he held on, by a very thin thread, as she tumbled once again into a shattering climax around him.

He let go too, then, allowing utter mindlessness to consume him completely, knowing that while the reprieve was welcome—greedily embraced, even—the gnawing, obscene hunger that continued to grow within him would still be waiting once this victory was absorbed.

That perhaps it would even be worse.

Because he was beginning to accept that things between him and Odessa might not be as cut and dried as he'd intended...

# CHAPTER SIX

'*KALIMERA.*'

The voice was close. Low and husky enough to draw from her a shiver, then rain down on every scintillating memory from last night and the early hours of this morning.

'You can pretend to be asleep, but your body betrays you,' Ares rasped.

A very unladylike curse spilled from Odessa's lips before she could stop it, drawing mocking laughter from the man whose arm circled her waist, pinning her in place.

'Good morning,' she said, cringing a little when her voice emerged far too husky.

Feeling heat rising into her cheeks, she pressed her face deeper into the pillow.

'Do you plan on ignoring me for ever?' he asked, just before his lips trailed down the shell of her ear.

Her shrug was a vain attempt at pretending she was un-affected, when deep inside her body was already rousing, melting for him.

'You'll have to excuse me. I'm not used to the morning-after thing.'

She wasn't sure what she expected when she chanced a furtive glance at him. It certainly wasn't for his humour to vanish…for his nostrils to flare in blatant displeasure.

She opened her mouth to do something stupid, like ask

him what was wrong, but Ares was already moving. She hated it that she immediately grew cold, craving his warmth.

Dragging the sheet up to her neck, she sat up.

He stood at the side of the bed, his narrow-eyed stare fixed on her.

'What have I done now?' she blurted.

He seemed reluctant to voice his thoughts, the rise and fall of his chest quickening as he stared at her. 'Tell me that idiot wasn't your first,' he grated out, hot Greek temper leaping wildly in his hazel eyes.

'You'll have to be specific. You seem to believe any man I interact with who isn't you or your father is an idiot or a bastard.'

'I only go on the evidence I'm presented with,' he said haughtily.

A shadow of amusement lightened his eyes. Then they hardened again into condemnation almost immediately, at whatever he was thinking.

'I mean Paolo Romani—that fool I saw you kissing on your eighteenth birthday. The man your father had been taunting me with for months.'

The reminder chilled her further. 'You saw everything?'

Her first mistake had been to throw herself at Paolo Romani in desperation. Little had she known that it had all been cleverly orchestrated by her father—that Paolo had been a willing participant in setting her up so that Ares would witness it. By the time she'd come to her senses, Ares was gone.

His features hardened further, his eyes no longer amused. 'I saw enough,' he breathed. 'You should thank your lucky stars that my father counselled restraint. I would've ripped you from his arms, then throttled you both.'

It explained a few things—although she suspected Ares hadn't seen the last part when, horrified with herself, she'd pushed Paolo away, then fought even harder when he'd pinned her against the wall. Labelled her a tease. It had necessitated her knee to his groin before she'd been able to make her escape.

More than discovering that Ares had seen that error of judgement, born solely out of desperate loneliness, confusion and defiance, it was knowing that his father had witnessed her behaviour too that made her cringe. 'Ares—'

'Did you enjoy it? Did he make you feel the way I do? The way I did back then?'

His words were like shards of glass, slashing at her to dig out secrets. Exposing truths she couldn't hide.

'No.'

His eyes narrowed, his body tight with tension. 'Don't lie to me.'

She laughed, the grating sound searing her throat raw. 'Trust me, I wish I could say differently. That it was the best kiss of my life. Then I wouldn't have hated you—and myself—so much.'

His gaze dropped to her mouth, then dashed back up to her eyes. 'He didn't hurt you, did he?'

*Not at first.*

'He was tepid. Boring.'

*He wasn't you.*

She didn't add that because, *Dio mio*, she'd exposed far too much of herself already.

'Well, one thing you're not when you're with me is bored, *ne*?'

His tone reeked of masculine arrogance. She hated the fact that it was well-earned. That he made every cell in her body shriek with excitement, breathless anticipation, and the feeling of living on the edge that adrenaline junkies craved.

It was almost addictive…in a way that made her fear for her emotions. Because it turned out neither time nor distance had shifted the gravity of how he made her feel. How eagerly she anticipated their interactions. How he drove her so effortlessly to the limits of emotion, then kept her poised there, in that heady space between despair and elation.

Odessa wished she could hate him for it, but the naked truth was that Ares Zanelis made her feel like nothing and nobody else had in her entire life.

'Can we be done with this? You have your answers. The kiss was boring. Romani wasn't my first. My first time, when it happened, was uneventful. I'm here now, with you. As you want. You should be happy.'

He wasn't happy.

Ares despised the unsettled sensations coursing through him two weeks after that far too exposing morning-after conversation. He'd let inconsequential demons get the better of him, and the enlightening recounting of her eighteenth birthday had taunted him with what he'd been denied.

Denied then, but fully enjoyed now, he tried reminding himself.

Why couldn't he be satisfied that the useless usurper Paolo Romani—the man Elio Santella had taunted him with—hadn't succeeded either. That, if anything, he—Ares—was the victor now? Why was he still disgruntled?

Because it felt hollow?

He'd put a ring on her. He'd strapped her down for the next five years, at least. So...*why*?

Because, as always with this woman, he craved *more*.

They'd settled into a routine in the fortnight since their wedding. He could run his empire from anywhere in the world, except on the rare occasion a face-to-face meeting was necessary. Leaving Odessa and his father on Ismene suited him just fine when he had to go away. And, yes, it helped that his new wife had taken an obvious liking to his island.

Also optimal was her eager welcome for him when they went to bed. He was nowhere near sating his hunger for her—which, again, was a good thing, since there was an end goal to all that sex.

What didn't satisfy him at all was that he'd been gone only forty-eight hours and his very skin jumped with need, like an addict denied a vital narcotic.

He rose from the seat on his plane, his restless gaze returning to his watch once more—as if he hadn't been checking every few minutes since he'd left London. He stopped pacing when an attendant approached.

'Can I get you anything, Kyrios Zanelis?'

'No, but you can find out how long before we land?'

'Of course, sir.' She returned in a minute. 'We'll land in fifty minutes.'

Fifty minutes. Then he could wrap her in his arms once more. Ensure the process of getting her pregnant was progressing smoothly.

*Is that all?*

*Yes!*

Nothing else mattered but that goal.

Except fifty-five minutes later his arms were empty and a clutch of dread lurked far too close to his heart.

'They've what?' he snapped at his housekeeper.

Demeter eyed him steadily, looking irritated, with her hands propped on her wide hips, her head tilted as if questioning his hearing.

'They took the car out half an hour ago. Kyrios Sergios said they were exploring the island.'

'The car. Not the buggy? Are you sure? Who was driving?' he snapped, dreading the answer.

Sergios had grudgingly given up driving because of his arthritis, but Ares knew he missed it dearly. If his father had talked his wife into taking out his sports car on unfamiliar roads...

'Was it Odessa?'

He was sure Demeter mentally rolled her eyes.

*'Ne,'* she confirmed.

'But she doesn't drive,' he replied, and even before a response was out of her mouth he was reversing his direction towards the front door and going to the garage where the sports car he rarely used should be.

It was a ridiculous idea to have a car on the island, but he'd given in to his father's passion for engines. And on the rare occasions when they transferred the car to his yacht and went to Mykonos or Santorini he enjoyed driving the streets with Sergios.

But there were strict rules to those arrangements.

He cursed under his breath as he stood staring at the empty space. Plucking his phone out of his pocket, he started to dial—just as the sound of a powerful engine reached him.

He whirled in time to see the yellow Spyder cresting the hill half a mile away, then zipping forward.

*Thee mou*, she was driving too fast.

Ares's legs propelled him down the driveway, so he could get a better view. So he could be driven out of his mind as he watched it jerk, then stall, before shooting forward once again.

His grip tightened around the phone, his heart in his throat. If anything happened to her...to them...

The urge to call out and tell her to stop the car immediately hurtled through him. But what if that distracted her? A cold shiver scrambled over his nape and for the next four minutes he stood stock still, watching the yellow speck grow larger until it appeared at the bottom of the driveway.

Then it stalled again, and he winced, feeling his teeth on edge as he heard the grinding gears. The car jerked once more, then sped up again, before coming to a screeching halt a dozen feet from where he stood.

Both occupants were grinning—but their expressions altered when they saw him.

*Kalos.*

He stalked towards her before the engine was turned off. 'What the hell do you think you're doing?'

'Hello to you, too,' she snapped back.

Ares refused to admit how good she looked behind the wheel. How good she looked, full stop. The Greek sun clearly agreed with her, and her tanned skin set off her startlingly beautiful eyes.

'I asked you a question,' he grated, residual terror unwilling to release its stranglehold on him just yet, even as other parts of his body reacted to the sight and heavenly smell of her.

'We went for a drive.' Her tone suggested she was stating the obvious.

He glanced at his father, his eyes narrowing when he saw amusement in his eyes. 'It's not funny,' he snapped at the old man in Greek.

Sergios raised both hands in mock surrender, then dropped a quick kiss on Odessa's temple before stepping out of the vehicle and making himself scarce.

'Is that scowl supposed to scare me?' she demanded.

He flicked at the button that elevated the gull wing door and held out his hand. 'Keys.'

She tossed them over with a glare.

'Get out. We'll talk about this inside.'

Her lips pursed, but she didn't respond when he caught her arm and led her indoors. His study was the closest room and he made a beeline for it, slamming the door behind him despite his attempts to control his temper.

He watched her take a seat on the sofa before the tall

fireplace, crossing her long legs and watching him with a composure he faintly resented as his senses leapt with the pounding reality of how much he'd missed her. How much even the thought of her being a little bit hurt had sent terror hurtling through him.

And he accepted that this situation was far from ideal.

Odessa watched him pace for a full minute. Then stop dead before her.

'Do you even have a licence?' he demanded. 'If I recall, your father forbade you from going near the garage. Women aren't supposed to drive, according to him, no?'

She flushed, the scorching reminder tightening her chest.

It was one of the many ways her father had limited her and kept her firmly under his thumb, before suddenly allowing her—in a rare display of magnanimity—to take lessons. Although he'd scoffed at the idea several times before her determination had finally worn him down.

'I do, actually,' she said, secretly pleased when she saw Ares's surprised look.

'And how many times have you driven yourself?' he tossed back.

She shrugged, self-consciousness dragging embarrassment through her. 'A few...'

'A *few*?' he echoed derisively. 'And how many of those "few" times included a vehicle with an actual engine and not the electric buggy you used to get around your father's estate?'

Irritation made her exhale sharply. 'Antonio let me drive his car to the shops once in a while.'

When her father hadn't been around.

'You mean Antonio the gardener, in his jalopy that barely went over twenty miles an hour before it threatens to shake itself into extinction?'

'What's your point, Ares? You don't want me to touch your precious sports car? Trust me, I've got that message. Or is it something else?'

'Something else?' he echoed coldly.

'You don't want me getting close to your father?'

Her heart squeezed as she said it. In a very short time she'd been reminded of Sergios Zanelis' inherent goodness and kindness, and in the last two weeks she'd found herself seeking his company, her yearning for the kind of father she'd never had alternately intensifying and being sated by the old man.

The thought that Ares might resent that sent a shaft of pain through her.

He sucked in deep, pent-up breath and she got the feeling he was trying to hold himself together. Why that both riled and excited her, she didn't want to delve into.

'Odessa, that car has more horsepower than a small plane. One mistake and you could've been…' He paused again, his eyes darkening as whatever thought he'd been about to express turned inward. 'Things could've gone very badly.'

A small gasp left her throat as she grasped his meaning. Shame engulfed her. 'I'm sorry, Ares. It didn't occur to me… I didn't think about your accident… Sergios was talking about how much he missed driving and I offered to take him. I should've—'

He jerked forward. 'I'm not talking about my father!'

This close, she saw his ashen pallor. Her heart leapt in wild giddiness. 'You were worried about *me*?' she whispered, stunned.

His irritation vanished with an exhalation. 'Does that surprise you so much?'

'Well…a little bit, yes.'

Something flashed in his eyes. Something like…hurt. It

was gone in a second, of course, but she'd seen it and her heart lurched.

'Ares...'

'Your health and safety aren't to be compromised under any circumstances. That's non-negotiable.'

*Non-negotiable.* Like their agreement.

Of course. His concern wasn't over *her*, but the possible child she might be carrying. The whole reason she was here in the first place.

'I didn't mean to jeopardise my position as your brood mare,' she threw out, anguish tinging her voice with acid. 'But I won't be wrapped in cotton wool, so you're going to have to accept that.'

He stiffened, but that flare of emotion in his eyes lingered, making her wonder if she'd read him wrong.

'Strike a balance between those two extremes and we won't need to have this conversation again,' he said. 'That includes taking out a supercar you can barely drive around an island with sharp bends and dangerous cliffs. Is that clear?'

It was maddeningly reasonable. She didn't agree immediately, because she wanted to keep fighting. She was still looking for a sign that he saw her as more than just the incubator contracted to carry his children.

'Odessa...?'

'Yes, Ares. We're clear.' She rushed to her feet. 'Can I go for a swim now? Or is that too dangerous, too?'

His expression relaxed, his hard edges easing a touch. 'Not at all. I'll join you. You taking risks on the road wasn't exactly the welcome home I was hoping for. We can both do with cooling off.'

Half thinking he would insist on his baby-making rights once they were upstairs, Odessa was oddly disappointed when he strode off to his side of their suite without looking back.

They arrived at the pool to find they weren't the only ones with cooling off in mind. Sergios was reclining on one of the loungers, peering over his bifocals at a car magazine. He set it aside when they approached, a smile breaking out when his gaze rested on her.

He said something to his son in Greek.

Ares glanced at her, amusement teasing at the corners of his mouth as he responded. Sergios laughed, then replied with something that made Ares's gaze probe deeper.

Odessa headed for the lounger next to Sergios, trying not to watch Ares from the corner of her eye as he tugged off the white torso-hugging T-shirt he'd changed into.

'You do know it's rude to speak a language someone in your company doesn't understand, right?'

Ares's smile stretched in genuine humour. It was beautiful and devastating to witness, robbing her of breath.

'That should be an incentive for you to learn my language quickly.'

She attempted a frown, to conceal the whirlpool of high emotions eddying through her. 'What did you two say?'

'My father said that the Greek sun agrees with you. I concurred and said you looked beautiful.' He paused, his eyes raking her face as her colour rose. 'And you grow even more enchanting when you blush,' he added, his humour lessening as heat and another emotion she couldn't quite fathom replaced it.

She reached for her sunscreen, just for something to do instead of gaping at him, and wondered at this dichotomy of hot and cold that set her senses spinning.

But was it hot and *cold*? Or hot and raw? Hot and savage? Hot and cynical? Hot and protective of his father and the baby she might be carrying? Was he staging a clever game, with the ultimate aim of ensuring he got the best of both worlds?

The uncertainty that had dogged her since she'd arrived, and was building with each day, threatened to smother her. She wasn't even aware that the bottle was slipping from her hand until Ares jack-knifed up, catching it before it fell to the floor.

Eyeing her with frowning concern, he swung his legs to the ground, poured a glass of refreshing juice and held it out to her. 'Hydrate,' he said.

She took the glass and drank—again just for something to do while her brain spun like a leaf in a tornado. When she couldn't settle her roiling emotions she stood, then threw off the thigh-length beach kimono that matched her caramel and gold bikini.

Stingingly aware of Ares's eyes raking over her every curve, she strolled to the edge of the pool and dived in, hating herself a little for enjoying how much she liked his eyes on her. How much she'd missed his presence in the two long days he'd been away. How eagerly she anticipated—with arousal pounding within her—the thought of sharing his bed again tonight.

She had no idea whether she was pregnant or not. Her period wasn't due for another few days. A simple pregnancy test while he was away might have solved the unknown, but she'd been reluctant to set the ball rolling.

Because she feared a positive result would mean the end of her presence in his bed?

Her heart lurched as the answer screamed in her head. Surfacing, she gasped in air—then jumped when firm hands closed on her waist.

'I was concerned you would stay under for ever. Or you had turned into a mermaid,' Ares drawled.

She turned, then lost her breath all over again when

the very sight of him, with drops of water glinting off his bronzed perfection, destroyed her breathing.

'So you came to rescue me?'

His teeth flashed. 'I came to demand the welcome I didn't get when I arrived home. Did you miss me?'

'Not at all,' she replied airily, ignoring the ache in her breasts and between her legs. Ignoring how utterly delicious and close his sensual lips looked. 'Your father and I kept ourselves entertained.'

His eyes darkened for a moment, then dropped to settle on her lips. 'Perhaps a reminder is necessary, hmm?'

She sucked in a breath, which made her breasts brush his chest, drawing a low groan from him.

'Ares, your father—' she started to protest weakly.

'Has dozed off.'

His legs tangled around hers, his hands pulling her closer until she was plastered against him. He lowered his head until his lips hovered tantalisingly, excruciatingly close.

'Kiss your husband, *agapitos*.'

With a helpless moan she surged forward that last fraction, pressed her lips to his, then shuddered in carnal delight when he immediately took over, sweeping his tongue over her eager lips before driving inside, tasting her with an erotic boldness bordering on aggression. An aggression she welcomed because—sweet heaven—Ares knew how to kiss her and drive her right out of her mind.

For long moments they kissed, deeper and deeper, with her arms clinging to his broad shoulders so she'd stay afloat. Against her belly his erection was imprinted urgently against her, a solid reminder of how he felt inside her.

Just when she thought she would be reduced to shamelessly begging for him to take her, right there in the pool, he eased back and broke the kiss.

Burnished eyes raked her face, satisfaction darkening his eyes at whatever he saw on hers.

'That's more like it,' he rasped. He dropped another hard, brief kiss on her lips. 'Unless we want to risk scandalising Sergios and the staff we'll have to pick this up again later. *Ne?*'

Still caught up in a whirlpool of sensation, Odessa simply nodded.

After a moment he released her, then swam a few laps before getting out. She knew he was watching from the lounger, despite his fingers flying over his phone. She tried to ignore him, swimming laps of her own in a wild bid to calm her senses, belatedly considering that she should have stipulated that these hot little *extras* were not part of their deal.

She hadn't. Now she was bearing the consequences.

Glancing over at him, finding his heated gaze still fixed on her, she knew deep down that she couldn't renegotiate. He would demand to know why. And she could hardly say she feared for her heart, could she?

She stayed in the pool until she risked turning into a prune. Until she breathed the tiniest sigh of relief when Ares's phone rang. Watching him pace away, keeping his voice low in consideration of his father, made her foolish heart trip again.

She insisted she was even more relieved when he sauntered back into the house. But she knew she was lying to herself. She craved the sight of him far more than she could comfortably admit. Knew she was nowhere near mastering how to stay aloof from Ares when she stepped out of the pool minutes later.

As she neared the lounger, she realised Sergios was awake.

He looked up, and although he attempted his customary

smile, she saw a shaft of pain dart across his face. Saw the hand he was trying to flex.

'Are you okay?'

He exhaled a vexed sigh. 'My body is reminding me that I'm an old man with old hands.'

Odessa glanced at the tube of cream Ares usually used on his father. 'Have you used your lotion yet?'

He shook his head. 'My son is caught up on one of his interminable phone calls.' He eyed her, then nudged the tube towards her. 'Would you mind?'

She reached for it, then paused. 'Are you sure you don't want Ares to do it for you?'

'He's not here. You are. And yours are softer hands than his,' he teased with a smile, then laughed when she blushed. 'You're my daughter now, *mikros*.'

Her heart squeezed, both with the deep yearning that assailed her and with the ache of wishing this wasn't a carefully orchestrated marriage with an end date hanging over her head.

*Unless she proved Ares wrong.*

Uncapping the tube, she squeezed lotion into her palm and then, reaching for his hands, slowly massaged it into his stiff fingers. His sigh of relief made her heart melt.

'I knew you would be perfect,' he said, then tossed her a cheeky wink.

Odessa burst into laughter just as heavy footfalls approached.

Ares froze when he saw them. His fierce expression made her fingers tremble. Sergios glanced up too, either oblivious to or totally ignoring the tension as he smiled.

'You're too late. I have a new apprentice. And, *ne*, before you ask, she's doing a much better job than you.'

Ares snorted at his father, but the look he pierced her with a second later was intense. Protective and probing far too deep. Odessa wasn't surprised at all when he pulled up a chair, sat down and proceeded to scrutinise every second of her ministrations.

If it wouldn't have risked upsetting the old man, she would have asked Ares to explain that look that seemed to say he possibly approved but was deeply wary too. She would have assured him that he had nothing to fear. That she wouldn't let him down.

'*Efkharisto, mikros,*' Sergios said, startling her.

'*Parakalo*, Sergios,' she responded automatically, her thoughts still consumed by Ares.

Ares drew in a sharp breath, covered by his father's pleased laughter.

'See? She's learning our language. Very soon she will be fluent.'

'So I see,' Ares responded a little gruffly. 'We should go and get changed. Dinner will be served soon.'

Again, he didn't coerce her towards his side of the suite when they returned upstairs, and throughout dinner he remained introspective, casting her heavy-lidded looks that slowly wound up her nerves until it was a relief to be done with coffee and dessert. To escape, despite knowing she'd still be dwelling on why Ares had seemed so eager to kiss her at the pool but didn't want to insist on his conjugal rights.

Had he changed his mind in the short time he'd been gone?

Unable to bear the tension any longer, she rose. 'I'm heading upstairs. Goodnight, Sergios. I'll see you in the morning.'

Ares's gaze bored harder into her, compelling her to look at him. When she did, his eyes raked her face, his hunger blatant.

'I'll be up in an hour.'

Her heart stumbled in her chest at the thick promise in his voice. Maybe he hadn't changed his mind...

She was berating herself for how eager she was, how she couldn't quite catch her breath because of the excitement fizzing in her veins, when he walked in.

His first words hacked that foolish excitement to pieces.

'My father is important to me, Odessa. Hurt him and you'll never know peace in this lifetime.'

Now her heart lurched for another reason, shrinking in her chest as she watched him prowl towards her. As much as it hurt to know he could think that of her, a part of her understood. She would have given her left arm to possess the kind of connection Ares and Sergios had with either of her parents. Would have protected it zealously with everything she had, the way he did with his father.

'I won't. I promise.'

Surprise flared in his eyes. His hands went to his shirt and he started to unbutton it with his gaze still fixed on her. 'You made another promise once. You broke it,' he drawled, almost reluctantly, his usual sharpness muffled. As if he wanted to wish it away but couldn't.

Maybe she could help?

She licked dry lips. 'Shall we talk about that?'

His gaze stayed on hers for a moment, before drifting down her body. 'Maybe later. Right now I'm in need of something else. Something that will guarantee our deal stays on track.'

Her nipples tightened at the raw hunger in his voice, even as her heart squeezed at his refusal to hear her out. To let her attempt to state her case for her actions all those years ago.

But he was tossing his shirt away, closing the gap between them with savage intent in his every step. And she could only draw a long, deep breath, hoping to replenish her lungs before he snatched it away. Because his hands on her body would do just that—drive her out of her mind until she didn't know whether she was coming or going.

He grasped her waist after discarding his loafers and trousers and picked her up as if she weighed nothing. A second later she was pinned against the bedroom wall, their faces a mere inch from one another as he speared her with his gleaming eyes.

'How eagerly your legs wrap around me... It's gratifying to see that in this we're on the same page.'

She hadn't even been aware she'd done it. That already her fingers were exploring his bare skin, her nails raking the hair at the back of his head, her core furnace hot and ready in anticipation of his possession.

The ease with which he derailed her thoughts and emotions fired up her spirit and her temper. She gripped a luxuriant handful of hair, tightened her hand until he gave an animalistic hiss and pressed forward, imprinting his thick erection deeper against her centre until her panties and his boxers might as well have been non-existent.

'If you don't want to hear me out, then maybe you need to stop talking and start acting.'

Her challenge fired him up, as she'd known it would.

His fingers dug into her buttocks, his eyes growing hooded as they devoured her mouth. 'Is that so? You're confident you're ready for me?'

'I know I am. In every way,' she stated bravely—even as her heart quaked and her instinct warned that there might not be much of her left by the time she came through this tempest.

That belief was scarily cemented when he thrust into her, powerful, hard and delicious, and had her screaming his name in under thirty seconds.

Then when it was all over, it had her clinging to him like

a limpet, unable to let go as they tumbled into bed. And she fell asleep with her head on his chest, her heart singing, because this was *exactly* where she wanted to be.

# CHAPTER SEVEN

OVER THE NEXT few days the unsettling possibility that whatever feelings she'd had for Ares in her teenage years hadn't diminished but had possibly intensified drove Odessa on restless, long walks around Ismene.

She was quietly awed by the extent of Ares's wealth, and the fact that, unlike her, he'd striven to fulfil his dreams, attaining impressive power and influence to boot.

As for his island—she accepted that she'd totally fallen in love with Ismene.

Where Alghero had been all vicious waves crashing onto craggy, dangerous black rocks and sheer cliff faces, Ismene had a few perilous bluffs and hairpin roads on the northernmost point, but was mostly white sandy beaches and a sea so calm and blue she suspected this was what heaven looked like.

She was sitting on one such bluff, enjoying the peaceful breeze in her hair, when her senses tingled. A moment later her husband's shadow fell over her.

'Odessa.'

Her head-to-toe shiver was so predictable, so damn Pavlovian, that she laughed quietly under her breath.

'Something funny?'

His low, deep voice rumbled through her. She delayed

looking up into his face, into those mesmerising eyes, for several seconds, although the compulsion soon grew unbearable.

'Until a few seconds ago I was comparing this to heaven.'

Most likely tired of her not looking at him, Ares crouched down to her level and, like clockwork, her focus swung to him.

His eyes probed. As always.

'And my arrival changed that view?' he asked.

She shrugged, watched his eyes flit to her bare legs before returning to her face. 'Well, Lucifer was once an angel, if I recall correctly.'

His mouth twitched. 'Which am I? Devil or angel?'

'Both? I think if any man can achieve the impossible, it'd be you.'

His head tilted the smallest fraction. 'Explain.'

Odessa couldn't quite account for the words that flew out of her mouth next. 'I begged you to save me. You did. Then you turned the situation back on me.'

His eyes darkened, and then a moment later his nostrils flared. 'You continue to give the impression that it will be a hardship for you, *agapita*.'

Her heart shrivelled. 'At what point in our past did I give you the impression that I'd be okay with abandoning any child I gave birth to?'

A muscle throbbed at his temple. 'So you still mean to prove me wrong?' he rasped, but the probing intensified, as if her answer mattered.

'Absolutely,' she hissed fervently.

After an eternity with his eyes locked on hers, his gaze snapped to the horizon. She followed it, her heart thumping hard in her chest. Part of her wanted to push away this important but sensitive subject, but a larger part of her loathed the thought of letting it remain unconfronted, like a festering wound. And, considering the news she needed to divulge about her possible pregnancy, she needed a moment. Because it felt larger than life…soul-shaking in a way she couldn't wrap her mind around.

*If* she was pregnant, then her life was about to change.

And if she wasn't…

How could she be bracing herself to mourn something she hadn't even contemplated this time last month? How could her heart be aching over the possibility that their activities hadn't reaped the desired results?

'What are you doing?'

She started, then refocused on where his gaze was locked on the sketchbook she'd brought on her walk. Heat flooded her face as his focus sharpened on her drawings.

'Nothing much. Just some doodling.'

'It looks like more than just doodling.' He held out his hand. 'May I?'

She shook her head, echoes of her father's ridicule rising in her head. 'I don't think so…'

'You think I'll mock you because others did? I'm guessing your father?'

Her chest tightened at this insight, but she didn't answer.

Nor did Ares put his hand down.

After a minute of silent battling, she reluctantly handed it over. Then drowned in mortified silence as he took his time to leaf through the two dozen pages. Just when she thought she'd die of embarrassment he raised his gaze. His expression—surprised, mildly shocked, *impressed*—choked her breath.

'You did all of this?' he asked.

'Yes,' she whispered, still not sure she wanted to hear what he'd say next. 'I know they're—'

'Seriously impressive?' he interrupted. 'Indeed.'

Her eyes widened. 'What?'

'I remember interior design was your passion.' His jaw gritted. 'Did he let you attend the college you wanted?'

*He?* Her father. *As if.*

'Of course he didn't,' she scoffed, and then felt a twinge for speaking ill of the dead. 'But I took some online courses on my own a few years ago.'

He nodded, his eyes still gleaming with surprise and warming respect. 'Good for you, going after what you want.'

Her heart lifted, prancing pathetically in her chest. Because she'd impressed Ares Zanelis, a multi-billionaire who owned some of the most impressive real estate in the world.

His gaze returned to the sketchbook. 'Speaking of what we want…' He handed the sketchbook back, but his gaze sharpened, drifting over to linger on her belly.

Odessa's heart lurched for a different reason, then squeezed at the thought of what she needed to divulge.

She sucked in a long, sustaining breath, her fingers tightening around the sketchbook now pressed to her chest, as if it might save or steady her.

'I don't know if I'm pregnant or not. My period didn't arrive yesterday…but I'm spotting a little today.'

The excruciatingly sluggish hours before she'd known she'd definitely missed her period had prompted a dizzying exhilaration—only to slide into horror when she'd spotted the blood. Even now, with the possibility that she might not be pregnant, Odessa clung to faint hope as she looked up at Ares.

To see hard, mercurial emotions flitting out of his face.

Bewilderment. Pride? Shock. *Fear?*

She shook her head. Perhaps she was deluding herself and it was all in her imagination.

'You're spotting, and you didn't think to mention it?'

His words emerged from a throat that was threatening

to freeze up with the surfeit of emotions coursing through him. They moved too fast for any one of them to establish supremacy.

He'd delayed asking her despite his every sense clamouring to know. He knew enough about the path to conception to know the odds of it happening so soon were improbable. And yet...

The unsettled feeling he'd carried since the morning after their wedding had gone, making way for other, equally alarming sensations. Disappointment. Desolation. *Panic*.

She pulled her lips between her teeth, her silver eyes shadowing before she answered. 'It happens sometimes with my period.'

'I see.' The words emerged clipped. Controlled. A direct opposite to what was going on inside him. 'What does that mean, exactly? That it didn't happen?'

The anguish darting across her face arrowed straight into him, making him realise the depths of his own expectations. And that she was equally affected. But then her chin rose in a way that would have amused him and made him proud had he not been stewing in peculiar sensations.

'I hope I don't need to remind you that it takes two to tango. Maybe we got the timing of things wrong.'

'Easy, *agapita*. As much as I wish to vaunt my virility, I know instant pregnancy isn't guaranteed, no matter how many times we have sex.'

Her shoulders relaxed a little, but her fight remained. 'Well... I...'

'Yes? You are expecting me to jump down your throat?'

She shot another fire-tinged gaze at him and his body responded. It was a call it apparently couldn't resist, no matter the circumstances. Ares was beginning to accept—resignedly—that it was a power he might have to concede to her. *Secretly*. It wouldn't do at all to make her aware of it...

'It wouldn't be unexpected,' she said.

Her meaning was clear. Stung more than he cared for.

'It seems you need reminding once more that I'm not one of those Neanderthals who blame their shortcomings on their women.' He shook his head, dragged his fingers through his hair, trying to gain some composure. 'Or am I wasting my time with that?'

She didn't answer immediately, and something shrivelled inside him.

Did she really think him a monster? *No*. He wouldn't lower himself into comparing what he was doing with what her father had done to her. He'd given her an option for freedom, for heaven's sake! And he continued to live with the unnerving, chest-searing sensations that recollection brought. The oddly stomach-churning possibility that she might exercise that choice in a few short years, despite her insistence to the contrary.

Elio, on the other hand, had treated his own daughter like a second-class citizen. A chess-piece he could move around his power-hungry board in ways that benefited him.

He crouched down to her level once more, wrapped his hand over her nape and tipped her gaze up to meet his. 'Tell me that's not what you think of me,' he demanded, and there was sensation that felt jarringly like desperation stirring in his gut as he searched her expression.

Her lips firmed and her eyes dug into his. Searching just as hard. 'Do you care what I think of you?' she whispered.

*Ne*. More than he suspected was wise.

'I can wait for that verdict.' He stood, held out his hand while digging out his phone. 'Come.'

She frowned. 'Where are we going?'

'You're spotting. That doesn't mean you're not pregnant. Let's go and make sure one way or another, shall we?'

She glanced down at his hand. Then, in another impressive flare of mutiny, she shook her head. 'Not until we discuss a few things.'

Harsh laughter seared his throat. 'I'm impressed, *agapita*. You have timed it perfectly to pull a stunt like this.'

'It's not a stunt,' she flashed back, her voice husky. 'I'm fighting for what I want. Even you must respect that.'

A part of him did. If he was being truthful with himself, the fact that she'd been born into an organised crime family and yet had managed to remain morally untainted had been one of his initial draws to her. Which had made her actions back then all the harder to swallow. And in light of Elio's clear manipulation of the situation, Ares had been teetering towards absolving her.

Now, his chest tightening anew, he curled his rejected hand into a ball and dropped it to his side. With his other, he dialled the number to summon his helicopter pilot, told him to ready the chopper for a trip to Athens.

The moment he hung up, she blurted, 'I'm not happy with granting you full custody of my child.'

An equally visceral need propelled a forceful answer from him. 'The original terms of the agreement stay. I can't risk my children going through what I did.'

She rose to her feet and brushed the sand from her dress with a grace so ingrained it was mesmerising to watch. Then she faced him, bold and unflinching.

'Ares, what your mother did to you and to Sergios was horrible. You have my word that I would never—'

'No,' he interrupted, the reminder of his lost sister and the parent responsible for everything he'd lost filling him with fury and bitterness. That Odessa would choose to bring it up...

He swallowed a growl. 'She swore too. I've seen videos of my parents together when they first married. They were ecstatic. She had stars in her eyes when she married my father and she vowed he was the love of her life.'

'Surely she didn't just change overnight?' she queried, bewildered. 'Something must have happened?'

He pursed his lips. 'My father thought she deserved the world and he wanted to give it to her.'

Odessa's eyes softened in that way they always did over his father. He was mildly jealous of it, truth be told.

'But she wasn't prepared for the long hours or his dedication to his job,' he went on. 'Nor, eventually, was she satisfied with being a chauffeur's wife, living in the shadow of all that Santella wealth.'

Recollection of the betrayal and pain he and especially his father had suffered dredged through him like spiked anchors, threatening to uproot his very soul.

'It took some time, yes, but their vows turned to ash. I watched my father bend over backwards and turn himself inside out to hang on to her. When he couldn't, he begged her to leave my sister behind. She refused. She took a helpless child she didn't really want because she knew how much it would hurt him. I can't… I will never permit that to happen to my own children.'

Mutiny etched deeper into her face and in the haunting eyes that threatened to condemn him. 'They're…they will be my children too! Doesn't that count for something?'

Hot on the heels of that unwanted trip down memory lane, the answer was dragged from his shattered soul. 'We've only just begun this journey, *agapita*. So the jury is still out.'

She reared back with a sharp exhalation, her eyes filled with anguish and fury. 'We may have just begun this journey, but you're quickly running out of road for goodwill, Ares. Keep that in mind.'

On top of the knots twisting in his stomach, he didn't appreciate the lance of guilt that impaled him.

And yet there it was, drilling deeper as she sailed past him, pale, defiant.

*Condemning.*

*'The jury is still out.'*

Odessa had no qualms about proving him wrong. And she would be damned if she'd wait five years to do so. Because as much as she'd endured in her life up till now, the reality of handing over custody of her child would completely annihilate her.

That urge to act sooner grew stronger the closer they got to Athens.

Beside her, Ares sat in brooding silence. With any other man she'd have attributed it to nerves, maybe even worry about what lay ahead of them. But he'd been steadily working on his tablet—although he'd rejected every call that had blared on his phone as the helicopter raced them towards the Greek capital.

Within an hour of landing they were in his doctor's office.

Odessa tried not to read anything into the inscrutable looks that passed between him and the doctor as she was thoroughly examined, blood samples taken. Nor did she let in hope when the doctor's seriousness lightened a fraction and Ares finally stopped pacing in the small but luxurious private room.

But by the time the doctor returned, after an excruciating half-hour, she was ready to jump out of her skin. So she didn't mind her manners when she heard the doctor address Ares in Greek.

'Tell me what's going on!'

Although she addressed the doctor, she couldn't drag her gaze off Ares, and the fact that he'd gone stock-still.

When she managed to look, she found the doctor beaming at her.

'As I suspected, the spotting is nothing to worry about. I wanted to double-check, of course, but everything is all right. Congratulations, Kyria Zanelis. You're healthily pregnant.'

She would've snapped that he could've told her that earlier, to save her going out of her mind, but the weight of his words snatched her breath and deadened her vocal cords.

She was pregnant. With Ares's child.

The child he intended to gain full control of the moment she stumbled.

Joy, panic and determination swirled like a vicious cyclone inside her as her gaze shifted to find Ares watching her with a ferocity that made every nerve in her body scream in confused, absurd exhilaration.

If she'd thought him possessive before, it was nothing compared to his expression now. It was almost as if he wanted to consume her.

She barely heard the doctor excuse himself. Her entire focus remained on Ares as he slowly prowled towards her, then stood examining her face for a moment before he slowly, inexorably, speared his fingers into her hair.

One hand cupped her jaw, angled her face up to his, while the other drifted down between her breasts, past her midriff to settle low on her belly, over the womb now cradling his seed.

'Mine,' he breathed.

She wanted to tell him he'd said that before, but it sounded flippant in the face of the seismic, life-altering reality unfolding between them.

'Ours,' she insisted, feeling that feral need to stake an equal claim on her child.

His nostrils flared and the possessive blaze in his eyes intensified. Odessa didn't back down. This was the most important battle of her life. And even as the warmth from his hand seeped into her belly, triggering a wild need to lean into his hold, their gazes continued to clash.

When he drew away she bit back a whimper, the loss of warmth so acute she shivered.

He saw the reaction, his eyes speculative.

Before he could probe that telling weakness, she turned away and snatched up the bag. 'Are we going back to Ismene?'

'Didn't you hear the doctor? He'd like us to stick around for a day or two, to make sure the spotting doesn't return. I also have some business to take care of in Athens.'

She shrugged. 'I was too busy watching your Neanderthal instincts attempting to consume you.'

For whatever reason, that produced a glimmer of amusement. 'And? Did they succeed?'

'That remains to be seen.' She glanced outside, to the sun-dazzled vista of Athens in the autumn sunshine. 'Are you going to growl at me if I say I want to take a walk out in the sunshine? Enjoy some of this hard-won freedom I've earned for myself?' she challenged.

Something stirred in his eyes. Want? A quiet clamour?

'I was going to suggest lunch. With me.'

The need to say yes was shockingly visceral. As was the caution not to give in to the insane urge to inhabit his orbit.

'I don't think I could eat anything just yet.'

Not until she'd digested the news that she was carrying a child.

Dio mio, *she was going to be a mother.*

She gasped when his hand's warmth returned to her belly, and he didn't try to hide the peculiar expression moving over his face.

'I don't want you getting heatstroke, so just one hour outside. Then the driver will take you home, and you will eat something, then rest. *Ne?*' he offered gruffly.

Odessa swallowed the emotions clogging her throat. *'Ne.'*

His eyes darkened dramatically, his gaze dropping to the mouth she'd used to answer in his own language. But perhaps she imagined the rough sound he made under his breath, because in the next moment he was grasping her hand, leading her out of the private clinic and into the back of the luxury SUV. Crisp instructions were issued to the driver, who nodded.

Fifteen minutes later they pulled to a stop outside a sleek six-storey building with a discreet Cyrillic 'Z' sign in silver at the top.

Ares's headquarters.

His gaze rested on her for an age before he said, 'Enjoy your walk. I'll see you at dinner.'

The moment he stepped out, Odessa wanted to call him back, to say she'd changed her mind about lunch with him. She pressed her lips together to stop exposing herself so completely, watching as his tall, imposing stride carried him away, several heads turning as his magnetism drew lesser beings to marvel at the god walking among them.

The vehicle pulled away and she found her own hand replacing Ares's on her stomach, awe tunnelling through a kaleidoscope of emotions. In less than nine short months she would be responsible for a baby. Would need to nurture it in a way she hadn't been nurtured. A way her mother hadn't been allowed to care for her because of her father's unreasonable archaic notion that a daughter was useless to him.

Odessa felt calmer knowing that, whatever its gender, Ares would do right by their child. His relationship with his father set her own heart at ease in that respect.

But not the fact that he prejudged her ability to be a good mother.

Was he right?

She pushed the idea away, desperately quashing the pain

that pushed into her chest. She would move mountains to ensure her baby's happiness.

'Where do you wish to go, Kyria Zanelis?'

The driver's question cut through the raucous jumble of her emotions. Taking a deep breath, she glanced out of the window. One god currently dominated her life. If she didn't stand to lose so damn much Odessa suspected she would give in a fraction. Okay, maybe more than a fraction. She was woman enough to admit to herself that she enjoyed Ares's earthy brand of domination.

But not with the stakes this high.

Noticing that the driver was still awaiting her response, she forced a smile. 'I want to play tourist for a while. Then maybe find a park?'

He nodded. 'Of course.'

Traffic slowed their journey, but it was worth it when they reached the Temple of Athena Nike. Even more jaw-dropping was finding Ares there, leaning against a powerful, gleaming black motorbike, his suit swapped for hip-hugging jeans, T-shirt and black leather jacket.

Every feminine nerve sprang to attention. 'I only just left you…what are you doing here?' she asked as she stepped out.

He shrugged. 'I've decided I'm a much better tour guide.'

She rolled her eyes at his sheer arrogance, while her insides strummed with unfettered delight. 'I thought you had work to do?'

He waved it away. 'My meetings can wait.'

He handed the driver the bike's keys in exchange for the SUV's and for the next hour proved his claim, offering titbits of history and salacious gossip she knew she'd never read in any history book. And because he was Ares Zanelis, he naturally had exclusive access at every monument, heightening an already unforgettable experience. And through it all he held her hand, drifted his fingers down her arm to direct her attention to where he wanted, pulled her close when other tourists invaded their space.

He called a halt exactly one hour later.

Stepping out of the SUV to admire the spectacular view from Lycabettus Hill, she ignored the tingling in her nape as she breathed in deep, smiling when her stomach started to growl at the tantalising scent of cooking.

'What's that smell?'

Ares smiled. '*Souvlakis*. Hungry?'

She nodded. 'Can we get some, please?'

'Of course.'

They'd stopped near a small park, with walkways interspersed with busts of gods set on pedestals.

Ares stepped out too. 'The vendor's just across the street. I'll be right back.'

Odessa had wandered over to the first pedestal when that tingling from before returned. Before she could turn to verify the source of her uneasiness her arm was grasped in a crushing hold, her captor frogmarching her towards the car park.

'Did you really think you could get away from me for ever?'

She shuddered at the cruel, too-familiar voice. And if the bruising grip hadn't been enough to tell her, she looked up into the livid eyes of Vincenzo Bartorelli.

'No, you can't be here—'

'Yes, I can. I have every right to retrieve my property.'

It was useless to ask how he'd found her. Men like him always found a way. What she needed to do was get away from him as quickly as possible—especially when the open back door of an SUV parked a dozen feet away revealed his intention.

Odessa didn't think twice about struggling, and then screaming as he yanked her towards the vehicle. She clawed at the hand imprisoning her, swallowing her mounting fear when he only dragged harder.

*Dear God, she was being kidnapped in broad daylight.*

If he succeeded…

If Vincenzo discovered she was pregnant with Ares's child…

The terrifying thought made her kick harder, her heart lurching as the open door loomed closer and the heavyset man standing guard advanced towards them.

Knowing that once he'd helped Vincenzo bundle her into the vehicle it would all be over, Odessa loosened her knees. She risked hurting herself, but he wasn't expecting a dead weight, and she momentarily slipped from his hold onto the baking pavement.

She'd bought herself mere seconds, but—

A vicious roar ripped through her thoughts. The scuffle, like everything else that had happened, took only seconds. Odessa didn't even have time to scream again before Vincenzo and his bodyguard were laid out cold.

She was struggling upright when strong arms closed around her, engulfing her with warmth and safety.

'Odessa! Are you all right?' Ares demanded, concern hoarsening his voice.

She nodded, her throat closing as she burrowed into him. 'Y-yes… I'm fine. I…'

'Shh, it's okay…'

Murmuring words in Greek, he moved his hands over her, stroking and soothing as approaching sirens rippled through the air. Minutes later, the authorities were carting away an incandescent Vincenzo.

Ares, visibly shaken, barely holding back his fury towards her attacker and his concern for her, watched as paramedics examined her.

From her struggle-tossed hair to her grazed knees and

the soles of her bare feet, he seemed to devour every inch of her in minute detail, his nostrils flaring as his gaze dwelled on the large rip in her dress.

With a single shake of his head, he gathered her in his arms. '*Thee mou*, Odessa…'

Her name was a command, a question, a declaration.

A shaken plea.

She shamelessly clung to the lapels of his jacket, her breath emerging in sob-tinged gulps. 'I'm f-fine…'

'I will be the judge of that,' he rumbled, in a voice so rough, so dangerous, a few passers-by exchanged nervous looks.

He ignored them all, his stride unwavering as he marched towards the SUV.

'But…the police—'

'They can wait until I'm good and ready.'

He buckled her in, his gaze once again roving fever-ishly over her before he shut the door with quiet, suppressed movements.

Settling behind the wheel, he gunned the engine and accelerated away, his jaw set in rigid steel.

He was clearly operating on a razor-thin edge. She wasn't going to be the one to tip him over. Hell, she was still shocked by Vincenzo's appearance.

'I can't believe Vincenzo is here…'

Realising she'd blurted her thoughts aloud, she cringed.

Ares's fingers tightened around the steering wheel and a growl rumbled from him. 'It was foolish of me to under-estimate how much he wanted you.'

The words were laced with regret and thick fury as he roared into the driveway of his Athens home.

Before she could think about exiting the car he was there, scooping her into his arms once again.

'Ares, I can walk,' she protested.

'I'm aware,' was all he said as he stormed through the front door, held open by his subdued, patently concerned housekeeper. A few other household staff lingered, but Ares ignored them, mounting the stairs two at a time and heading straight for his suite.

There he set her on the edge of his bed, then strode off towards his bathroom.

With a minute he was back, minus his jacket and shoes.

The sight of Ares crouched before her, his face set in rigidly bleak lines as he slowly pulled off his T-shirt, snatched at her already fractured breath.

He tossed it away, then without a word spoken grasped the hem of her dress and started to draw it up.

Her hands flew to cover his. 'What are you doing?'

A flash of distress crossed his granite features. 'I need to see for myself that you're unharmed. And I'd really like to wash that bastard's touch off you. Are you going to fight me on this, Odessa?'

The intensity in his gravel-rough tone juddered through her. And, since the second part was what she wanted too—what she would've done had she been alone—she shook her head.

Mere seconds later the dress was off, and he was tossing it away. Her bra and panties followed, and then she was caught in the sizzling net of his thorough scrutiny as his hands and eyes raked every inch of her body. When he reached the grazed skin on her knees, a garbled sound left his throat. His eyes were near-feral before he sucked in a calming breath. Still he muttered words under his breath she was sure weren't meant for polite company.

Rising, he scooped her up again, tucking her high against his chest, his eyes locked on hers.

'This is the second time he's put his hands on you. There won't be a third,' he vowed, with a dark rumble forged in fire, brimstone and retribution.

# CHAPTER EIGHT

ODESSA WAS TOO consumed by the sensation of his near-naked body against hers to form words. And, really, what could she say that wouldn't tip this man still hovering on a dangerous precipice over the edge?

Was it only a few hours ago she'd teased him about his Neanderthal tendencies? She was witnessing them in full effect now. And, since they both needed time to come to terms with a day filled with glorious highs and disturbing lows, she let him work his way through his emotions.

He did that by first cleaning her grazes and then, leaving his boxers on, urging her beneath the warm shower. He washed her with a gentleness that brought another lump to her throat, quickly washing himself thereafter. Then he towelled her hair dry and wrapped her in a soft, thick cotton robe.

Once again taking her in his arms, he returned to the bedroom.

A tray had been delivered while they were in the shower.

Ares placed her in the middle of the bed and tugged the covers over her just as his phone began to ring. He glanced at the screen, and grimaced. She followed his gaze, saw it was his father.

His reluctance to leave her evoked a melting sensation she couldn't for the life of her harden. But perhaps it was okay, just this once, not to fight it so much. To bask in his care and attention to ease her ordeal.

'It's okay. Answer him. I don't want him to worry.'

A layer of his tension visibly evaporating, he nodded.

Their conversation was mostly in Greek, but Odessa didn't mind. It gave her time to collect herself, to permit the hovering relief that she was safe. That her baby was safe.

A soft sound left her throat as she collapsed against the pillows, unable to quite shut out the worst-case scenarios whizzing through her brain. Her hand sliding over her belly, she sent up a fervent prayer of gratitude that none of them had come to pass.

It took a moment for her to realise that Ares was silent. That his gaze was fixed on her, and the same emotions she'd felt were reflected in his face.

She struggled upright, her heart thumping at the force of his reaction. An emotion she absolutely didn't want to read into for her own peace of mind.

'Is he okay?' she asked instead, deflecting the heightened atmosphere between them.

A rough, bewildered sound left his throat. 'You're asking after him when you should be concerned for yourself?'

She shrugged. 'He's a worrier. And I suspect it's not fun when the people you care about are in trouble, but out of your reach. Besides, I can multitask quite well.'

Her attempt at humour fell flat, but she was beyond caring. What absorbed her attention was Ares, ambling closer, that gaze never straying from her for a second.

'No, it's not fun,' came Sergios's disembodied voice.

Her jaw dropped when she realised the call hadn't been concluded. Ares's mouth twitched as he held out the phone.

'He wouldn't hang up until he'd seen you.'

She took the phone, her smile wobbling a little when Sergios's worried face filled the screen.

'*Mikros?*'

'I'm fine. I promise.'

He nodded, but the reminder of what he'd been through was reflected in his sombre eyes. 'It's my turn to say a prayer for you, like you did for me five years ago.'

She inhaled sharply. 'How do you know about that?' she whispered.

'Know about what?' Ares enquired.

She pressed her lips together, shaking her head at Sergios.

His was warm, benign, his smile all-encompassing. 'Tell him, *mikros.*'

She raised her gaze to Ares. 'When I found out about the accident I said a prayer for your father,' she confessed, and then, after a moment, she added, 'And for you.'

Myriad emotions flashed across his face, too quick to read but all heavily weighted.

'She did more than that. She lit a candle every morning and every night. And she petitioned the staff to do the same.'

Mortification and panic at this exposure of her emotions weakened her. 'Sergios…'

The old man shook his head at her protest. 'No, my dear. I won't be quiet about it. You defied your father to spend hours in the chapel, praying for me and my son. He deserves to know it.'

Her face heated and emotion clogged her throat, sending prickles to her eyes.

Ares's eyes flared, searched harder, then blazed with whatever emotions were moving through him. 'Is that true?'

'Do you want it to be?'

He looked poleaxed for a second, then fiercely intent. 'Answer the question, Odessa.'

'Yes. It's true,' she confessed in a whisper, dragging her gaze away, because the reminder of those three awful weeks when his life had hung in the balance was still viscerally heart-wrenching and something she didn't like to revisit often.

He took the phone from her, said a few words to his father, then ended the call. 'Look at me, Odessa,' he commanded, his voice gruff and uneven.

She raised her head, boldly met his eyes even though she wanted to run. Shield herself from further exposure.

But that wasn't what she witnessed. He looked…nonplussed. Unsettled. And, probably for the first time in his life…uncertain.

As if she…Odessa…had shaken his foundations.

'Why?' he rasped after several heartbeats.

Several unguarded reasons rushed to the tip of her tongue. She barely managed to bite them back. She'd revealed too much already.

She pursed her lips, debating not answering, then… 'Because, whatever you think of me, I'm not a monster.'

For an eternity, he simply stared at her. Then he rose, strode away to the other side of the room. She should have been relieved he was dropping the subject, but all she felt was deflated. Then that charge he carried with him, that sheer vitality, infused her again when he reversed his course. Kept coming until he reached her.

Crouching beside the bed, his eyes teeming with the indecipherable emotions he seemed to be grappling with, he reached out, brushed his fingers down her hot cheek. 'You're many things, *agapita*. Some I'm yet to fully discover, because it seems you can throw a wrench in my beliefs, but one thing you're most definitely not is a monster.'

He stared at her for another age before, leaning forward, he dropped a kiss on the corner of her mouth.

'*Efkharisto.*'

'*Parakalo,*' she answered, the response natural and automatic now.

But inside she was a mess, and the feeling that they'd turned a corner was unwilling to leave her frantic brain.

'I can't believe Sergios got the butler to tell him about that,' she blurted, eager for a distraction.

'He cares for you,' Ares said, his tone gruff.

That melting feeling grew warmer. Comforting. But it lacked something vital. Something she was fearful to hope for.

'I know.'

'He wants to return to Athens. I told him not to.'

She nodded. 'It's not necessary if we're going back to Ismene soon.'

A look crossed his features, too quick for her to decipher. Then he was placing the tray on her lap.

'You never got around to eating,' he drawled.

But she caught the trace of wicked humour in his tone. He, too, was attempting levity.

A small chuckle broke free before she could stop it. Then she curbed it when she heard the tinge of hysteria tingeing it.

Her eyes widened when she saw what was on the plate. *Souvlakis.*

She wasn't going to question how this had been whipped up so quickly. Maybe it was relief, residual adrenaline, or knowing she was eating for two now, but her stomach growled again as the aromas hit her.

Folding warm bread around the slices of meat and gooey sauce, she bit into it.

At her soft moan of appreciation, Ares's eyes darkened.

He watched her eat two, then nudged a third towards her when she hesitated. She took it, eating more slowly this time.

When she was done, he removed the tray and tucked the covers over her. He watched her for another second, then brushed a kiss on her temple. 'Rest now.'

The combination of life-changing news and the awful

event that had followed had sapped her energy, and although it was barely evening, Odessa sagged against the pillows, her eyes already drooping by the time Ares's broad form disappeared through the bedroom door.

She slept fitfully, her rest disturbed by choppy dreams. Twice she felt hands soothing her, running through her hair, calming her as she fell back into sleep. When she woke a few hours later it was to find Ares pacing the terrace outside his suite, the phone plastered to his ear as he conducted a low, heated conversation.

Sensing her regard, he ended the call and entered.

'Is everything all right?' she asked.

He glanced down at the phone with a frown, then slotted it into his pocket. 'Not entirely, but I'm working on it.'

'Was that the police?'

He hesitated for a second, then nodded. 'The police chief is a friend. He's assured me that the idiots Bartorelli hired to assist him have ratted on his intention to kidnap you. He also made the mistake of committing the crime in Greece, not Italy. He has significantly less sway in my country, and I've ensured that his assets are not available to him. Your uncle, too, has been put on notice that if he lifts a finger to help Bartorelli he stands to lose substantially. Not that he needed much persuasion... Bartorelli out of the way suits him just as much as it does me.'

The speed of his retribution while she'd been asleep made her grip tighten on the covers. Was it the same swiftness with which he would remove her from their child's life?

'So, in essence, you threw your weight around?'

His arrogant nod was unapologetic. Determination blazed high and formidable in his eyes. 'Indeed. And I won't hesitate to throw even more around to get what I want.'

*For her or for his child?*

While she knew the feminist in her should rail against it,

for the sake of keeping her child safe Odessa fully embraced that ruthless fortitude. But she vowed to herself that if—when—he attempted to use it against her, she would fight with everything she had. For now...

'For what it's worth, thank you,' she said.

For some reason her words drew a dark frown, which he visibly shook off as he perched on the side of her bed. Her breath caught as he reached out to brush back her hair and caress her cheek.

'How do you feel?' he rasped.

Odessa swallowed before she could speak. 'I'm fine. I'm glad it's behind me.'

Again, shadows chased across his face. Then he stood. 'Is there anything you need before we leave?'

Reminded that they were only supposed to be in Athens for her appointment, she shook her head.

'*Kalos.* We'll leave within the hour,' Ares said, and then, with another prolonged look, he returned to the terrace.

She got up and, ignoring the discomfort in her knees and arm, went to her own side of the suite.

Her ruined dress had disappeared—thankfully. Going to the closet, she selected a pair of wide palazzo pants and a white batwing top made of cotton so soft and luxurious Odessa was certain it had cost the earth.

But it covered her bruises, and with her deepened tan the colour looked good on her, and she greedily took the boost it provided, sliding her feet into heeled gold mules before adding gold hoops to her ears. A quick brush of her now dried hair before containing it in a loose bun, a spritz of her favourite perfume, and she was ready.

Returning to Ares's suite, she momentarily panicked—until she saw her bag and the sketchbook tucked into it.

Ares was waiting in the foyer when she came downstairs, his gaze latching on to her as if he needed to read her every expression. Odessa's face reddened and, forcing her gaze away, she smiled reassuringly at the hovering housekeeper.

Outside, the sight of an additional SUV full of mean-looking bodyguards made her grimace.

'Is that really necessary?' she asked Ares.

A grasp of her hand, which he settled on his thigh, then a solid, implacable 'yes' was all she got.

Until, after staring out of the window as the SUV by-passed the helipad and headed for the private side of the airport, she turned to Ares as the vehicle stopped in front of a large, sleek-looking jet.

'Why the jet? Are we not taking the chopper to Ismene?'

He shook his head. 'No. Change of plan,' he stated grimly.

'Are you going to tell me what that plan is?' she demanded when he didn't explain.

His face was shuttered for longer this time. 'Did you like it on Ismene?'

Unable to deny it, she nodded. 'Yes.'

'Then be assured you'll like where we're going just as much. Maybe more.' He held out his hand and beckoned her. 'Come.'

Intrigued despite herself, Odessa took a deep breath and went.

Several hours later, she turned a full one hundred and eighty degrees on a lush green lawn, unable to catch her breath at the beauty that surrounded her.

They'd flown south, to the island of Zanzibar. A slice of heaven just off the coast of Tanzania, to her it had been a paradise destination only ever longingly explored on a map. Until now.

The long journey from the airport, with the windows down in their Jeep, had given her a breathtaking glimpse of the exotic island that offered an intriguing blend of African, Arabian and European cultures.

Like on Ismene, Ares's sprawling villa was poised on a glorious beach. But, unlike on Ismene, the swaying palm trees that bordered the Zanelis estate, the powdery white sand beneath her feet, the turquoise beauty of the Indian Ocean, the promise of exploration of coral reefs and the knowledge that there were now a few thousand miles between her and Vincenzo washed away her worries.

Well…most of them.

Ares had grown more brooding, insisting she rest, and absenting himself when she refused. And, unlike on Ismene, they didn't share adjoining suites. A sombre part of her turned downright despondent when she discovered that his suite was in the opposite wing from hers.

Deliberate or unintentional?

Odessa wanted to berate herself for reading too much into it, but since nothing was settled between them, and her instincts were clamouring more strongly than ever, she couldn't very well dismiss it.

And yet, over the next few days, every time she tried to broach the subject Ares knocked the wind out of her sails by snapping out of his mood and displaying the same disarming gentleness he'd provided the evening of her attack.

It toyed with her heart and emotions, making her doubt her own inclinations.

Thoroughly fed up, it drove her into his study a week after their arrival.

He'd left to make some work calls after their light lunch overlooking the ocean. But lying in bed, her senses refusing to settle as she stared up at the heavy saffron silk canopy surrounded by dreamy white muslin curtains that made up her gorgeous four-poster queen-sized bed, she'd suddenly snorted her impatience at herself and searched him out.

Botticino marble floors cooled her feet, but her palms were clammy when she lifted her hand to knock, her heart thumping hard in her chest when his deep, roughly husky voice answered.

He sat behind a desk, building plans and files strewn all over the massive surface.

'Odessa.' Her name was tinged in surprise as he rose and met her halfway. 'I thought were going to take a nap.'

'So did I. Turns out I can't sleep when I have things on my mind.'

His brows pleated. Taking her hand, he led her to an armchair. Thinking he wanted to see her seated, Odessa was once again disarmed by his sitting down and settling her in his lap.

'What things?' he asked.

Up until then, she hadn't even known how to broach the subject, or what to bring up first. Turned out her psyche was fully prepped.

'Would you have sent me back to Vincenzo and Flávio if I hadn't agreed to have your baby?'

He tensed beneath her, but she refused to take back the question.

'That doesn't matter now,' he said.

'But it's not a no. Or a yes. Would you really have sat back and watched Vincenzo force me into marriage?'

Face set, his fingers absently brushed the almost faded grazes on her knee. If he sensed that it toyed with her breathing, he didn't give any sign of it.

'No, I wouldn't have sent you back,' he admitted after a tight stretch of silence. 'Does that satisfy you?'

She tried to stop her heart from singing. She failed. 'Yes, it does.'

He caught her wrist and tugged her close, until she tumbled against his chest. Then his fingers spiked into her hair, training her attention on him.

'Don't think that gives you any upper hand,' he rumbled in warning.

'I wouldn't dare.'

His eyes narrowed. 'Why do I suspect you don't mean that? That you're simply saying what you think I want to hear?'

It took monumental effort to curb the smile fighting to slip free. Just as it did to remain still within the magnetic forcefield of his arms.

'Because you have a very suspicious mind?'

'Stop wriggling,' he growled, his eyes dark and smouldering with so much heat she wondered why she wasn't engulfed in flames.

'Then let me go,' she countered.

He didn't.

Instead, those eyes dropped to her mouth, and a groan slowly rumbled from deep within his chest. His lips parted and his warm, minty breath washed over her.

Everything tightened within her in howling anticipation. But just when she thought he'd claim a kiss, devour her in the way they both so blatantly wanted, Ares released her.

Her limbs were too leaden for her to scramble off his lap as fast as she'd fallen into his hold. Or perhaps it was the sting of rejection, despite her visceral awareness of his arousal pressing hot and heavy against her hip?

'Do you not want me any more?' she blurted, before she could stop herself.

He stiffened, his eyes darkening dramatically. 'What gives you that idea?'

'Besides the very obvious altered sleeping arrangements?' she scoffed, although her voice emerged a little shaky.

For a long time he remained silent, his eyes hooded, his jaw set. Then he exhaled harshly.

'You were attacked, *agapita*. Right under my nose. On

the day I found out you are carrying my child. The day I discovered you prayed for me when I was…incapacitated. I feel that does indeed alter things a little between us.'

Her heart lurched. Did that mean he'd changed his mind about her?

'In what way?' she asked, hope making her breathless.

His hands returned to her hips, tightened on her flesh momentarily before, almost reluctantly he released her again.

'At the very least I don't want to visit my…needs on you. Unless you expressly wish me to.'

'So you're saying the bedroom ball is in my court?' she ventured, at once touched and disappointed.

It was a hard thing for the domineering man she knew him to be to admit to, thus explaining his recent brooding. But Ares, after several moments, gave a grudging nod.

*'Ne.'*

It wasn't entirely what she'd hoped for…but it was progress. She could build on it. And, while she wanted to throw caution to the wind and jump his bones immediately, she managed to rise, stay steady on her legs as she walked to the door, keenly aware of the need pulsing between her thighs.

But, more than that, she was entirely too conscious of the warmth burrowing deep into her heart. Those two profound sensations should have kept her moving, and yet her feet slowed at the door, her hand braced on the frame as her body pivoted to face him.

'Ares?'

His eyes darted up from where he'd been staring at her bottom. *'Ne?'* he responded gruffly, the faintest flare of heat colouring his cheekbones.

'For what it's worth, I appreciate you coming to my rescue then, too. Thank you.'

For the longest time he simply stared at her. Then he nodded abruptly, jerking forward and reaching for his tablet. 'Close the door on your way out,' he rasped.

She left with her heart only just a touch more at ease. And, yes, she did realise how easily he'd regained the upper hand.

There were more subjects to discuss, of course. But they'd resolved one. She had over eight months before the baby came. The remaining obstacles would be tackled in time.

The tiny voice that taunted her, saying that she was burying her head in the sand, she strongly ignored, heading for the kitchen.

Most of the French doors and windows were thrown open during the day, letting the light, salty breeze weave its magic through the room. Odessa breathed in deeply and entered the kitchen, a strong yearning filling her heart.

The resident chef looked up, his friendly smile turning a touch wary, then almost comical as she relayed her request.

She was elbow-deep in her preparations when her skin began to tingle. She didn't need to look up to know who was striding towards her. His scent alone easily gained superiority over the aroma of rich bechamel sauce and ragu.

For a long moment Ares leaned against the marble counter, only raising an eyebrow to address her when her compulsion to look at him won.

'What are you doing?' he asked.

'What does it look like? I'm making lasagne.'

'I have a house full of staff, including a Michelin star cook. Whom I'm told you have sent away?' He looked around, his brow twitching at the mild chaos around him.

'Yes, I did. He's French. He doesn't make lasagne like my mother did.'

'Your mother?' he echoed, with a slight softening in his eyes.

She nodded. 'It's one of the few memories I have of us,'

she whispered, then shook off the shaky emotion. 'Anyway, she used a secret recipe I intend to pass on to my son or daughter. I can't have your chef around.'

She passed her hand over her stomach and his expression changed again. He looked disarmed. Shocked. *Affected.*

But a moment later his feelings were back under tight control, his gaze sliding to the melting, mouth-watering bechamel and the meat sauce bubbling gently on top of the stove. His tongue slid to the tip of his lower lip and Odessa was sure he didn't realise he was doing that.

She curbed a smile and didn't revel too long in the satisfaction welling inside her. Picking up a spoon, she scooped up a taste of sauce, blew on it, then held it up. 'Try it.'

He tasted it, and cursed under his breath.

She bit her tongue to keep from smiling openly. 'Is it that bad?'

His mouth twitched. 'It's adequate.'

'Hmm… Well, I'm guessing that's why you're licking your lips?'

He harrumphed. And Odessa knew she was at high risk of being lost when she realised that she thought it the sexiest sound in the world.

He remained silent as she finished layering the pasta and sauces and slipped it into the oven. Then… 'Is this to be a regular occurrence?'

'Why? Let me guess… You're going to object to me lifting a finger?'

He shrugged. 'Lifting a finger, no. Exerting yourself too much, yes.'

She sighed. 'I'm not going to be lounging about drinking fruit punch and demanding pedicures for the next nine months, so kill that idea immediately.'

Deeper amusement flitted over his lips before he shook his head. 'I didn't think you would be. But I have an idea.'

She paused in tossing the salad, setting the tongs down almost warily. This was the first time they were having a conversation that wasn't either fraught with past recrimination or thick with sexual tension. It was almost…congenial. So much so Odessa was concerned the slightest wrong move would shatter it.

She followed his gaze to the timer on the oven clock, then he held out his hand.

'We have time. Come.'

Her wariness morphed into a different sort of apprehension. They hadn't touched properly recently, besides the occasional brushing of fingers when he helped her up or down the stairs. Deliberately holding his hand felt…far too intimate.

He started to frown.

Not wanting to lose this lightness between them—because it was new and, yes, because she wanted it to remain a little too desperately—she slid her hand into his.

The almost pained glance he sent their clasped hands a moment later swelled a sensation far too close to her heart.

She was still grappling with it when he walked her into his study and over to the mini-conference table set beneath the window across from his desk. As she neared it, she saw several miniature replicas of Zanelis buildings.

As impressive as they were, it was seeing her sketchbook on the table that rattled her.

'I had it brought down,' he said as he intercepted her expression.

'Why?'

'Because I could use your drawings—if you're willing to share your talent?'

Her heart jumped into her throat, along with surprise and shock. 'Really?' she echoed, her voice husky with overflowing feelings.

His nod was brisk, and yet he studied her with his usual intensity that said he was invested in her response. 'They're too good to sit around collecting dust.'

The fervent yearning and joy gripping her was almost overwhelming. She tried to tamp them both down. Her life had so far been a series of wrenching transactions sucking at her soul and her emotions.

*'Behave and you'll not be punished.'*

*'Atone for not being born male and you'll be spared my wrath.'*

*'Make friends with this family so we can benefit.'*

*'Marry me and I'll save you if you have my children...'*

Sure, the first part of the deal with Ares had been at her instigation. Was this offering now out of the goodness of his heart? Or was there a hidden agenda?

'You're overthinking it,' he said when the silence lengthened.

'Am I?' She saw his eyes darken. She waved a dismissive hand, hoping her torn feelings weren't plastered on her face. 'Okay, tell me what you mean.'

He stared at her for several seconds before nodding at the tallest structure. 'My latest project in Abu Dhabi will be completed in six months. The top forty floors are residential, including five penthouses. The remaining floors are retail and business. My team is in the process of headhunting interior designers. I can tell them to stop searching if you're willing to take on the job and work from here.'

Her jaw gaped, and then she shook her head. 'I couldn't— You—' She bit her tongue as heat rose in her face.

'Speak your mind, Odessa.'

'You don't need to throw me a bone just because I'm carrying your child.'

His lips twisted, half amused, half sardonic. 'I didn't

get where I am today by making decisions based on senti-mental whims.'

Why didn't that surprise her?

'So you're not worried about being called out on pos-sible nepotism?'

A conceited shrug moved his muscled shoulders. 'I'm in the prime position of being rich and powerful enough not to care what people think of me. And you being this worried means you'll provide a premium service. The job is yours if you want it.'

She almost swallowed her tongue. 'Just like that?'

'Ne.'

The confirmation was simple. Immovable.

Several seconds passed, and then, registering he was se-rious, she stared down at the perfectly crafted miniatures. Luxury skyscrapers. Warehouses. A sports complex or three. Whole streets of residential properties with cute little parks.

They all had names—seemingly with a theme she couldn't quite fully grasp yet—except for the building he'd just been talking about.

'What's this one called?' she asked, more to give herself time to digest his offer and feel how much her heart yearned to embrace it than anything else.

When he didn't respond immediately, she looked up to find a quizzical expression. As if she'd caught him in an uneasy, vulnerable moment.

A moment later, his jet lashes swept down. 'I haven't decided yet.'

Odessa suspected that wasn't the complete truth, but since she didn't want to add to the tumult now occurring inside her, she let it go.

'So?' he pressed a minute later.

She gulped down the knot building in her throat. 'I... I'll put together some samples and we'll take it from there.'

He nodded. 'Good. But that means allowing the chef back into his kitchen to do his job, yes? I suspect he'll throw a tantrum if he's kept away much longer.'

Odessa couldn't stop the smile that tugged at her lips, or the buoyant feeling that built and built inside her as she returned to the kitchen, Ares prowling lazily behind her. Or the simple contentment that gripped her when he devoured a helping of her lasagne and immediately demanded seconds.

She couldn't escape the pressing confirmation that her feelings for her husband were far from platonic. Hell, had they ever been?

With the no echoing in her head, she admitted, too, that his offer just now had touched her more than she'd expected it to. For the first time in her life she was embracing a true sense of accomplishment that was reawakening the fire in her soul.

The career and the family she'd only ever dreamed of was creeping tantalisingly closer...

There was still the problem of Ares's deep mistrust and full custody plans hanging over her head, but she decided with a firm promise to herself that she would tackle that too. Or at the very least put contingencies in place in case she needed them later.

Because the subject of her child—her *children*—was too precious to leave to chance.

# CHAPTER NINE

*Six months later*

ODESSA ACCEPTED THAT she shouldn't have left things to fester for this long.

Because unlike her pregnancy, which had sailed along smoothly after a few weeks of morning sickness, the atmosphere between her and Ares had stagnated into tepid politeness—with the occasional bout of wild lovemaking when her need built and built and then drove her into his bedroom late at night. There they slaked their lust with a wild fervour that mocked their daytime interactions, that mocked the emotional barricades she'd fought so hard to put up. Because Ares, for all his consideration, remained immovable over their agreement. Had coolly shut her down the handful of times she'd tried to broach the subject.

Sergios had lightened the atmosphere when he'd joined them on the island. Or maybe they'd just stepped up their pretence of a happy marriage...

But she suspected Sergios wasn't fooled...his shrewd looks missed very little.

And now Odessa's increasingly anguished heart had finally cracked, and she was unwilling to let sleeping dogs lie any longer.

Starting with an hour-long confidential consultation with

a lawyer who reassured her that she'd have a good case to petition for shared custody of her children, should it come to that.

Any flashes of guilt she felt at proceeding with that meeting, she pushed away. If anything, she was simply taking a leaf out of Ares's book. He'd gone to great lengths to draw up an agreement to distance her from her children. She had every right to seek her own counsel.

And, yes, she also acknowledged that she was praying it never came to that.

That hope burned in her heart as she made an appointment to see the lawyer when she returned to Athens. Since Ares had written into their agreement that his child was to be born in his country of birth, she anticipated they would be returning soon.

Now, as she lay back in preparation for the last scan before the baby came, her hand travelled over the hard bump of her growing baby, seeking comfort from her baby as she'd been doing increasingly over the last couple of months, once her figure had changed and the reality of motherhood had become irrefutable.

Ares entered the guest suite, and she braced herself for what the sight of him did to her. He ruined her in the best possible way every time she grew weak with need and sought his arms. So much so that she feared she was past the point of effectively guarding her heart any longer. Especially when his gaze raked over her, lingered on her belly and his nostrils flared with open, unfettered possessiveness.

'Are you ready?' the female doctor asked, smiling. 'Maybe today we might be lucky and get to discover the sex, yes?'

Ares settled himself beside her, as he'd done both times before, his piercing gaze fixed on her. 'You still want to know?' he rasped.

'Yes.'

He nodded.

The doctor went to work, passing the wand over her swollen belly.

The moments before their baby's heartbeat echoed in the room were heart-stopping. The second it did, and the 3D image appeared, Ares slid his fingers between hers. That was a first. The electric sensation of their palms touching, an act only usually replayed in bed, made her breath catch, made her wonder if their peculiar stalemate was fracturing. Whether this was the opportunity she needed to take.

'I'm happy to report your baby boy looks completely healthy,' the doctor announced.

Ares inhaled sharply, his eyes growing fever-bright as they latched on to the screen, then swung to her a moment later.

She blinked, her own eyes prickling as he leaned over and brushed a kiss over her temple. 'He's beautiful. As are you,' he murmured.

Her fingers tightened within his, her racing heart screaming everything she wanted to say and was terrified to.

The doctor's following words barely registered, but Sergios's entrance into the suite broke her momentarily out of the urgency biting at her.

'A healthy grandchild is all I have prayed for,' he said. 'But I am looking forward to teaching my grandson a thing or two about classic engines,' he added with his customary eye twinkle. Then his expression grew serious. 'Along with a few life lessons about not repeating your mistakes. You know?'

His stare bored into his son's, then drifted to her. It was the most pointed he'd ever been, and that urgency dug into her harder.

Which made it all the more disconcerting when she tracked Ares down two short hours later and saw the open suitcase.

'You're leaving?'

She hated how much her voice shook. How hollow her chest felt already. It was a testament to how she'd grown to long for his scraps of occasional affection that she'd mourn his absence.

He looked up, his fingers tightening momentarily on one of the ultrasound photos they'd been given. 'Yes.' His lips tightened. 'I'll be back in a few days.'

She lifted her hand to brush back her hair, and the tanzanite bracelet and marching necklace she'd crafted at a local jewellery workshop should have reminded her how much she felt at home here. Today it only reminded her of how long she'd been in this gilded paradise. That its beauty couldn't take the place of what her heart truly craved.

'Okay, this has gone on long enough,' she told him. 'How long do I have to stay here?'

He tossed another shirt into the case. 'Until your safety is guaranteed.'

'And until then, what? We're going to keep playing this hot and cold but mostly cold game?'

She almost wanted to laugh at how bewildered he looked. Then she wanted to grieve. Because this level of ignorance meant she didn't mean as much to him as her heart yearned to.

'What are you talking about?'

*Dio*, she hated how steady, how utterly commanding he was, while she floundered so desperately. The only time Ares seemed to be moved by anything was when it pertained to her pregnancy. Or when her needs got the better of her and she sought his touch.

Well, she was sick of it. And also sickened that this conversation needed to happen.

'You can barely look me in the face. When I enter a room, you leave within minutes.' Her voice choked. 'You're showing the traits of my father, Ares. And, yes, you might find it offensive to be compared to him, but that's my only yardstick. And guess what? It's just as deplorable when you do it.'

His face lost several shades, and even his eyes snapped in affront. 'Odessa—'

'No. I won't live like this any more. Tell me what I've done or I'm leaving—even if I have to swim a hundred miles to get to land.'

He dragged his fingers through his hair. 'I gave you a choice. You made it clear you would use it—use *me*—only sparingly. I'm guessing I have your pregnancy hormones to thank for that consideration?'

Her jaw dropped. 'Wait… Are you accusing me of using you for s-sex? I didn't see you complaining when—' She stopped, her face flaming.

His hands raked through his hair, then he shrugged. 'Something is better than nothing, I guess.'

Her mortification grew. 'Ares…'

His face tightened at whatever it was he heard in her voice. 'I don't require your pity or—'

'That's good, because I wasn't about to offer it,' she snapped, and then the greater need to settle this once and for all drove her closer to him. She almost reached for him, but a lifetime of rejection loomed large, so she kept her hands balled at her sides. 'Look, can we agree that sex isn't really our problem?'

He stiffened, his eyes narrowing, but she caught something on the edges of his expression. Anticipation? Hope?

'Then what is our problem?' he asked.

She pressed her lips together, then made the plea. 'Have faith. In me.'

*In us.*

The unspoken words dislodged a tightness in her chest. Her hand found its way to her belly again, reminding herself what she was fighting for.

'That history won't repeat itself.'

His eyes blazed as they dropped to her stomach. For a blind moment she was sure he would say something. But then he turned away, his movements jerky as he finished packing.

'I need to go to Abu Dhabi to see to the final arrangements for the tower. Vincenzo's sentencing is also this week. I need to be in Athens.'

She'd forgotten about that. After months of delay and attempts to weasel his way out of jail, Vincenzo had finally pleaded guilty, eliminating the need for Odessa's presence at his trial—an outcome she suspected Ares had made happen. But, while her heart attempted to melt, because he'd saved her that ordeal, too, she still needed to fight her corner.

'Once he's officially behind bars we can discuss you coming back home.'

Her temper ignited at that. 'You're talking as if I need your permission to leave. I don't remember agreeing to being carted off around the world at your whim.'

He went rigid, but the fingers clutching his case betrayed him, his knuckles turning white at her response. 'This isn't a whim, Odessa. And you're wrong. Our agreement says differently.'

She inhaled sharply. 'Excuse me?'

His lips twisted. 'You need to read the small print. I have the right to take you with me wherever I go in the world. My business is global. How else would I get you pregnant if I didn't have you with me at all times?'

'I'm already pregnant,' she said, stating the *very* obvious.

He shrugged. 'Doesn't change the wording of the agreement.'

Cold invaded her chest, shrivelling her heart. 'Why are

you doing this? Surely you can't still believe that I'm an emotional threat to this child?'

He opened his mouth, but she beat him to it.

'Nothing! I have done nothing wrong in the first place. You're judging me by impossible standards. I'm human. I'm bound to make mistakes.'

'Not with my children you won't,' he seethed.

'Enough, Ares! I kissed a boy who wasn't you when I was eighteen! And I said some things I didn't mean to my father about you. Are you going to punish me for ever for those two things?'

'No,' he growled, stepping up to her and blotting the sunlight, so all she could see and all she could feel was him. 'But—'

He gritted his teeth.

'But what?'

'You made me yearn for things I couldn't have.'

Her mouth gaped open. 'Things like what?'

His own lips parted, but he said nothing. They breathed the same roiling air for a minute, before he slashed his hand through the air.

'It doesn't matter now.'

'Of course it does. I'm being judged for something I didn't even know you wanted from me. At the very least I have a right to know, don't I?'

His gaze dropped to the ultrasound photo, which was at risk of being crushed between his fingers. When he locked eyes with her once more, the flash of bleakness she saw strangled her breath.

'Fine. You made me *hope*. Until I saw you in another man's arms, I thought that the words and promises we'd made to one another meant something.'

'They did.'

His eyes narrowed, his judgement scorching her where

she stood. 'Tell me, then, *matia mou*... How would you have felt if our positions had been reversed and my tongue had been down another woman's throat, her hands touching parts of my body the way you wanted to touch me? Would you have brushed it off as a simple mistake?'

Her throat clogged, blocking any answer she'd hoped to give. It would've killed her. And, God, she didn't know whether she would've forgiven him. But...

'I'd like to think I wouldn't have condemned you for the rest of your life,' she whispered, the part of her that insisted he was better than this stubbornly clinging on to hope.

That hope grew when he lifted his hand, traced a thoughtful path down her cheek, then was shattered conclusively with, 'Ah, but then I'm Greek, *agapita*. The fires of retribution burn brighter and hotter within me. Now, enough of this. Whatever rows unfold between us, you remain the vessel carrying my child. I won't have your health harmed.'

That was as definitive as it could get. No matter the highs and the lows, Ares would see her first and foremost as a brood mare.

Waves of pain at his words crashed through her, leaving her unable to catch a full breath.

'Do you even hear yourself? Who refers to the mother of their child as a "vessel"? You know what I think? You don't hate me for kissing someone else under some misguided notion of self-preservation. I think you're afraid to reach for what you truly want. You want to guard yourself against all future pain. That's fine. But do you have to be cruel to me to achieve that?'

For the first time in her life she saw Ares Zanelis totally nonplussed. His mouth gaped slightly and extreme bewilderment filled his expression.

After a handful of seconds, he shook his head. 'I didn't mean—'

'Yes, you did. And the sad thing is you don't even realise how hurtful you're being. Or that you don't need that stupid wall you've erected around yourself. Why don't you do us both a favour? If you can't be the kind and considerate man I know lives in there somewhere, maybe you shouldn't come back at all.'

The words seared her very soul as she uttered them and Odessa stopped breathing, the visceral fear that she'd said words he might act upon lighting a terrifying blaze in her heart that threatened to annihilate her.

His eyes widened, shock slashing through the bewilderment. And, hell, if that wasn't the saddest, funniest and most heartbreaking thing she'd seen in a while.

For the first time Ares was rendered speechless.

And somehow she found the strength to accept something else her foolish heart needed to know. It was time to guard her heart. Because months…years of this would be untenable.

She took one step back. Then another.

Her eyes narrowed as he jerked forward, as if caught by the strings of her emotions.

As she took her third step he stopped himself, features shuttering.

He remained there, a pillar of ruthless fortitude, watching as she silently begged him not to let her go, but knew he wasn't going to stop her.

Wasn't going to do anything but leave.

A week later, she summoned a smile for Sergios as they sat down to play chess, infusing enough enthusiasm into the smile for his contemplative looks to lessen, but not totally dissipate.

They hadn't discussed his son's absence, but she knew he wasn't pleased about it.

*Join the club...*

She wanted to blame those hormones Ares had mocked for missing his body next to hers in the dead of night. She'd tried telling herself she'd been through worse, after living under her father's ruthless commands for almost three decades, but her heart taunted her.

*You knew early enough that Elio didn't love you. He made no bones about the fact that he'd have preferred a son to a daughter.*

With Ares, her heart had refused to believe for a very long time. Now that hope was gone. But she needed to keep her vow front and centre in the heart that was now being pulverised by the realisation that she'd never got over Ares Zanelis. That despite the almost-decade that had passed he'd remained the ideal in her mind and her heart. She feared he always would, but she needed to put that fear aside. For her child's sake.

'I'm old, *mikros*, but not so old that you should pretend to play badly enough to make me feel good about winning,' Sergios griped.

Her gaze snapped to his, guilt riding her about spacing out. At his droll look, her eyes dropped to the board. In three short moves she was about to forfeit the game.

'Oh, I'm sorry...'

He waved her apology away, but while his customary humour lurked in his eyes his expression was surprisingly solemn. 'Don't be sorry, *mikros*. Do something about it.'

She started at his direct, gritted tone. Surprised that for the first time she was catching glimpses of where his son had inherited his steel from. Sergios might couch his interactions with humour, but at his core he was implacably loyal. Fiercely determined.

'I...I don't know what you mean.'

His mouth twisted, the motion so reminiscent of his son

that her breath caught. 'Yes, you do. Only you're wallowing when you should act.' A flash of anguish marred his weathered features. 'If I'd acted sooner, instead of remaining stubborn back when things were unravelling in my own life, perhaps things would've turned out differently for my family.'

She reached over the table and covered his hand with hers, swallowing the lump in her throat. In the context of her own pregnancy and already loving her baby more than life itself, she couldn't fathom going through what he'd endured.

'Sergios, I'm—'

He patted her hand. 'You mean well, I know. But I'd much prefer you direct that sentiment somewhere more proactive.' His gaze dropped to her belly, and there was an expression of fondness and pride in his gaze when he lifted it back to her face. 'My grandson deserves the happiest home you can provide. And, no, I don't mean the one you're contemplating, separated from my bull-headed son should he not pull his act together.'

At her visible shock, he snorted.

'I'm not blind. You two pretend all is well for my sake. I wish you'd save all that effort for fixing things before they're irreparably broken. Or do you not want that?' he challenged, again with that blade of ruthlessness that made her understand once and for all that she'd sorely underestimated Sergios Zanelis.

'I… Yes, I do.'

He squeezed her hand. *'Kalos,'* he grunted, then his smile reappeared. 'Now, give me a better game. Who knows? Strategic thinking might help you devise how to bring my son to heel.'

They played three more better, challenging games. And she went to bed that night with a slightly altered plan than she'd woken with that morning.

She couldn't shake Sergios's urging. Nor the spark it had ignited. As she pulled the covers over herself the urge to win the most important game of her life burned bright.

Brighter.

Ares had accused her of making him hope—something his mother's actions had clearly eroded. What if that hope wasn't misplaced? What if she had the power to make them both happy beyond their wildest dreams?

The strong kick in her belly just then made her gasp, then smile in the dark. At least she had one person in her corner. Well, two. Ultimately, Sergios would support his son in whatever decision he made, but for now she could siphon strength from the only father figure she'd truly known.

She wouldn't just fight for her children.

She would fight for her husband too.

That spark turned into a conflagration less than a minute into the video conference calls with Ares's team after breakfast the next morning.

'We're thrilled to have you on board the design team for Odessa Tower, Mrs Zanelis. Your designs are quite breathtaking,' the team leader gushed.

She sucked in a breath. 'I'm sorry...what did you say?'

Nervous glances met hers. 'Did I say something wrong?' the woman asked.

'No,' Odessa said hurriedly. 'I just didn't catch the name of the property, that's all.'

'Oh...it's called the Odessa Tower. Is that not correct?'

Her fingers tingled, and then the sensation rushed through her until her whole body was engulfed. The memory of Ares's evasive look flashed through her mind. He'd named his latest project after her?

When he didn't care for her.

As a taunt, it felt too cruel to contemplate. But could it be…?

The seductive whisper suggesting that it was something else, something she'd yearned for all her life, was too big, too weighty, to dismiss.

She had people waiting for her, giving her strange looks that prodded her to get her act together fast or risk the very thing she'd questioned Ares about. The last thing she wanted was to leave the impression she had no clue what she was doing. Even if it was somewhat true.

Clearing her throat, she pinned on a smile. 'No, you're right. And I'm glad to be on board too. Shall we get started?'

The white-knuckle determination to succeed in her first ever venture kept Odessa focused on the meeting when every cell in her body wanted to examine every facet of what she'd just learned.

*Ares had named his latest project after her.*

Because he wanted to perpetuate the ruse that theirs was a genuine marriage? No, she couldn't make that argument stick either. Ares had no need to prove himself beyond the bounds of making his father happy.

And yet…

Odessa sucked in a steadying breath, attempting not to be even more disarmed when they settled on three of her designs for the mega-penthouses along with two more from other designers. She struggled not to gape in wonder at the initial 3D projection of how her work would look when it was completed, in time for the official opening in four short weeks.

'Mrs Zanelis?' the team leader prompted hesitantly, clue-ing Odessa in that she'd been staring, agog.

Cringing, she offered an apologetic smile. 'Forgive me.

I was just marvelling at how efficiently you've all worked to produce this.'

Her praise did the trick, drawing pleased murmurs which carried through to the end of the meeting.

The moment she signed off, her hands flew to her mouth.

After a good five minutes of trying to absorb the news, trying not to let her heart soar at the connotations of it, she brought up a search engine on her laptop, her fingers tapping out frantic requests.

With each revelation her breath shortened further.

Every Zanelis project and iconic piece of real estate held a significant meaning to *her*.

Sapphire Island. Her favourite gem.

Gemini Place. Her star sign.

Occhi d'Argento. Silver Eyes.

Odessa Tower.

She stopped after the tenth one, her heart shedding the last of its protective barriers. Perhaps she was wildly over-exaggerating the importance of all of this. But if she wasn't… If Ares had even a shred of feeling for her over and above her role as his long-term incubator…

Before she could change her mind she reached for her phone, her fingers aiming for the number at the top of her contact list.

'Odessa.'

His voice was deep and resonant, rumbling through her being to settle in a place she was beginning to suspect would always be reserved for this man. The truth of that shook through her, forcing her to grip the phone tighter.

'Is something wrong?' he demanded, his voice sharper.

She started to shake her head, before she remembered he couldn't see her. That the fact threatened to make her giggle took her by alarming surprise.

Grappling her wayward feelings under control, she responded. 'No, there's nothing wrong. But… You named your new tower after me?'

Even from thousands of miles away she sensed his wariness.

'Ne,' he said after an age. The silence stretched out before he added, 'We're trying to create an image, aren't we? It made sense.'

Her heart plummeted, and then a wave of anger took over, thankfully shrouding the swell of hurt. 'Made sense to who? Because if that's the true reason—'

'Why wouldn't it be?' he interjected, with what sounded like a touch of defensiveness.

Which—absurdly—made her feel fractionally better.

'Because firstly, you didn't consult me, and secondly, you're forcing me into more pretence.'

Again, silence reigned. Then he sighed. 'If you must know, it was the first name that entered my head.' His tone had morphed into gruffness and clear reluctance. He hadn't wanted to admit it. 'Nothing else made sense after that.'

Her grip eased, her breathing turning shallow as elation bubbled once more beneath her skin. 'I see.'

He cleared his throat. 'But—'

'It changes nothing. I'm aware,' she slotted in, before he could.

But his protest was useless. He'd admitted the truth. And the vice around her heart was easing.

'Was that all?' he rumbled. 'I have a busy afternoon.'

The urge to put her plan into action bit at her, but Odessa didn't want to do it over the phone. This was too important.

'No, that's all.'

*For now.*

Expecting him to ring off, she held her breath when he lingered.

'You're well?' he asked.

*No. I miss you more than I can express.*

'I'm well,' she said instead. 'So is the baby. I'll see you soon.'

She hung up before he could query that. Before he could talk her out of it.

Standing, she left the study, eager to put thought to action immediately.

Sergios stood outside the door. His gaze probed, hard and direct, and again Odessa wondered how she hadn't seen this side of him before. Perhaps she hadn't wanted to see it? Examine what it might mean to her?

She answered the question in his eyes. 'I'm leaving, Sergios. As soon as it can be arranged.'

'And your destination is…?'

'Abu Dhabi is wonderful at this time of year, I hear,' she said.

His smile was immediate and approving, the hands that gripped hers warm and firm. 'Good, *mikros*. Very good.'

# CHAPTER TEN

THE DEEP PEACH dress with silver piping did very little to hide her pregnancy.

Not that she was trying to. On the contrary, Odessa loved nothing more than to smooth her hand over the soft chiffon and her swollen belly, her heart kicking when she felt movement beneath her touch.

Her much-enhanced cleavage did draw a blush to her cheeks—especially the way the silver piping moulded and emphasised her breasts, cinching beneath her bust before flaring to the floor. She loved the way the three silver rope spaghetti strap design emphasised her tan. Her hair, left to grow even longer over the past few months, was caught in an elegant chignon, a few sun-streaked highlights gleaming in the dark caramel tresses.

A nervous smile curved her light peach-glossed lips, and no matter how long and deep she inhaled, she couldn't quite catch her breath.

Because of what lay ahead of her.

Odessa wasn't entirely sure it was a good idea to combine the grand opening of Odessa Tower with attempting to put her marriage on the right track, but she'd made the decision and was determined to stick to it. Not least because the past four weeks had been hectic, with Ares cagily resisting her every attempt to find ten minutes to talk.

As if she'd conjured him from thought alone, she sensed him in the doorway. Nerves held her still and she didn't turn around immediately. Instead, she tried to compose herself, to think through how she would convince him to give them a chance.

*If he said no...*

Her heart lurched, but she pushed the feeling away.

If he said no, she'd have no choice but to revert to her initial plan to meet with her lawyer and fight for her children.

But, *Dio mio*, with every fibre of her being she hoped he didn't.

*Thee mou*, she looked glorious.

A delicious peach—pun very much intended—that every atom of his body screamed at him to devour. He hadn't paid much attention to the changes that happened in pregnant women until his own wife had fallen pregnant. He should have. Because over the months he'd been bombarded with surprises. Some unpleasant stomach-churning when her morning sickness had hit full-force and nothing had seemed to alleviate it. Then the very absorbing, carnal and viscerally *primal* impact of watching her body change. Seeing her belly swell with his child.

He understood now how some men were rampant with protectiveness.

A pregnant Odessa was sexy on a level that continued to baffle and flay him—which was why he'd grasped those nights she'd graced his bed with desperate hands. Until he'd ruined even that with his careless words.

Ares wasn't ashamed to admit he was both thrilled with and dreading her making good on her promise not to remain in Africa.

*Ne*, he knew he had a battle on his hands—he could see her determination to take him on brewing in her eyes. His mistrust had hurt her, and his past pain still had a stranglehold on him that was in danger of shattering his marriage.

But he'd face that battle soon enough.

At almost eight months pregnant she positively *glowed*. Her stylist had aced her appearance with that shade of peach. And the way the silver set off her beautiful eyes and the bodice hugged her breasts...

She spun from the floor-length mirror to face him, and Ares realised he'd groaned under his breath.

He straightened from leaning against the archway that led to her dressing room, silently watching her putting the finishing touches to her attire.

Shimmery silver earrings dangled from her ears, drawing his hungry gaze to the long, graceful line of her neck. With a savage punch of arousal he remembered that erogenous zone. His shaft hardened and his mouth watered.

Angling his body so his tuxedo hid the evidence, he forced his gaze from her breasts to her face. 'We need to get going. Are you ready?'

His voice was husky and rough, and he watched heat flow up her gorgeous face. Biting back another groan, he locked his knees to stop him from charging across the room and tasting that erogenous zone once more. He feared it would be just the start.

'Yes...' She lowered long, beautiful lashes and swept up her silver clutch. Then she darted another look at him. 'Do I...?' She laughed and shook her head. 'Never mind. I won't have time to do anything about it even if I *don't* look okay.'

A hard bark of laughter left his throat. 'You're joking, right? You'll be the most beautiful woman there tonight.'

Her stunning eyes grew wide. 'Thank you. You don't look so bad yourself.'

The smile that teased her lips snatched the rest of his breath away. For a moment he was thrown back to the girl who'd broken her father's rules and ventured into the forbidden part of the estate. The girl who'd hung around the garage, not afraid to get herself dirty while she washed the cars with him and his father. The girl he'd placed on a pedestal…which he was beginning to suspect was her rightful place after all.

'Ares?'

He realised he was staring and caught himself, smoothly holding out his arm in silent command. She glided towards him, a goddess. And, hell, even the silver points of her heels playing peekaboo with her hem was sexy to him.

Could anyone blame him?

They hadn't made love since she'd uttered those two words that had shaken him to the soul. That had made him turn tail and flee, despite yearning to reach for her.

*Have faith.*

He deserved every second of this suffering.

'Are you sure you're all right?'

He clenched his teeth, then failed immediately to resist. He pulled her scent into himself once more, tortured himself with the glorious softness of her skin.

'I will survive,' he clipped, then tossed up a prayer that this would prove true.

For some reason that response sent a dart of hurt across her face. A common occurrence, he admitted, his own mood plummeting. Because this too was his fault, wasn't it?

Hell, he seemed to have lost his way along this journey.

Stances he'd taken had left him tossing and turning at night until he was certain he was being driven out of his mind. And for the first time in his life he was avoiding his own father, because the old man didn't fail to let him know by word or look how he was failing. Hell, Sergios had uncharacteristically called him a fool earlier on today!

Silence reigned until they were approaching the lift.

Then she looked around, searching for the very man in his thoughts. 'Is Sergios not coming with us?'

'He claimed he didn't want to intrude, so he went ahead an hour ago.'

She sent him a searching glance. 'You don't believe him?'

Despite his inner turmoil, his mouth twitched. 'He's visited the tower twice and the restaurant three times this week alone.'

She smiled, taking his breath away. 'He's excited.'

'*Ne*. He boasts to everyone who will listen that his daughter-in-law decorated the tower.'

Her stunning silver eyes widened. 'Really? But I only designed a fraction of it.'

'An important fraction to him. To me,' he tossed in after a second.

He sensed her gaze on his face, and with a compulsion he couldn't resist he met hers.

'To you or to your team?' she asked, a touch hesitantly.

'I am my team.'

*And your husband.*

Eyes still clinging to his, she swallowed. He wanted to trace the line of her throat with his fingers so badly he had to clench his fist to kill the temptation.

Because he was becoming painfully aware that he'd taken a wrong turn somewhere along this journey. That he'd clung for far too long to slights that had been out of her control. Her care and affection towards his father these last few months had been eye-opening. And even while they'd been apart she'd thought about them, prayed for him. The way she'd cared for herself and their unborn child during this pregnancy...

If he'd caused her irreparable harm—and he was fearing he had—did he deserve her?

The question shook him to his core, his whole body jerking in reaction to it.

'Ares?'

He shook his head, feeling a rare panic—the kind he'd experienced only once before, when Bartorelli had seized her in Athens—crawling over his skin.

He'd been dealt with once and for all, thankfully. But what now? Would he succeed this time around? Or was he fated to let her slip through his fingers like she had all those years ago?

He glanced down at her, attempting to harden himself against impending pain. Because if he failed...

'Everything is fine,' he reassured her, despite not believing a word of it.

He could fix things. *Couldn't he?*

Those two words plagued him all the way to their destination—his greatest business achievement to date.

Ares stepped out after they'd pulled up to the red carpet leading into the tower he'd spent three years pouring his vision into. He ignored the intense flashes of cameras as he helped Odessa out, and then he simply couldn't pull his gaze away as she stared up at the structure he'd named after her.

He'd wanted something unique, to stand out against the many stunning masterpieces of the Abu Dhabi city landscape. The end result far surpassed his exacting expectations.

Set entirely on a raised concrete platform, surrounded by a shallow lake that jetted plumes of water into the air, the soaring sixty-floor O-shaped design was set in ten concentric silver mirrored rings, each a reflection of her stunning eyes in every mood. Powerful spotlights lit the structure from below, while strategically placed lighting silhouetted it beautifully against the night sky. Reflections from the rippling water made the whole building glimmer, seeming to move in hypnotic beauty.

Not unlike the woman next to him.

Ares hadn't quite known—or perhaps had readily accepted—his subconscious's intentions when he'd selected the colour, but now he did.

Everything he did was influenced by her in one way or another.

It was time to stop fooling himself that she wasn't important. That all he wanted from her was the child she was carrying and the other children she'd agreed to provide him.

It was time to *have faith*.

Every other outcome left a searing hollow in his chest that intensified the panic gripping him.

'I've never seen it at night-time. It's even more breathtaking,' she said, her voice low, husky.

Perhaps it was not meant for his ears alone, but he couldn't help hoping it was.

'*Ne*, it is,' he agreed, not shying away from the throb of emotion in his voice.

The flash from another camera drew her attention from his building and he was both irritated by the distraction and a little jealous of her open admiration for what he'd built.

He wanted her to look at *him* that way. Not to see the layer of wariness in her eyes when she glanced at him.

He wanted to be done with this opening that had attracted some of the most influential people in the Middle East and from around the world, all of whom wanted a piece of architectural history.

A deep sense of urgency gripped him all through the launch, but he throttled it down. Odessa, along with the design team, deserved her due for a magnificent job.

Pride filled him as he listened to gushing accolades about

the decor his wife had helped create. As he watched her blushingly accept her due.

*His wife.*

That thing shifting and settling within him as he thought of her not as the woman carrying his child but as the woman he'd once imagined making a life with felt heavy.

Moving.

Significant.

And right.

*Have faith.*

*Yes.*

It was a huge relief when he claimed her four hours later, tugged her arm once more into the crook of his and firmly stated that his pregnant wife needed to rest.

'Thanks for that,' she murmured as he walked them towards the magnificent doors and into the foyer of the tower. 'My feet are killing me and my back feels as if it's made of concrete.'

He led them into the lift and pressed the button marked *'Odessa Penthouse'.*

'Then you won't mind if we spend the night here and go home tomorrow.'

'So we get to break in the tower?' she asked, eyes wide. And then a heated blush swept into her cheeks. 'I mean...'

He laughed, welcoming the brief relief to the churning unease in his gut. 'I know what you mean, *eros mou*. And, yes. We'll be the first to spend the night in Odessa Tower.'

His voice felt thick from the arousal surging through him, and he didn't bother to hide it. She looked infinitely delicious, and the hunger sweeping through him was fast reaching untameable levels.

It was both a relief and a torture to step into the privacy of the penthouse. Relief because he had a little breathing room to think, and torture because for the first time in his life he was terrified of how the next hour would go.

They stepped into the spacious and lavish caramel, silver and gold living room in time to see the night sky explode in bright colour.

'Oh, I forgot about the fireworks!' Odessa exclaimed.

Suppressing a groan, Ares crossed over to the extensive liquor cabinet and poured a glass of alcohol-free champagne. Returning to where she stood at the floor-to-ceiling windows, he handed it to her, and then, simply because he couldn't help himself, he trailed a hand down her jaw and neck, fighting the punch of emotions as she shivered and swallowed.

She wasn't immune to this, he reassured himself. She'd boldly told him she'd prove him wrong in their agreement. That he'd regret it. And he did now. Surely it wasn't too late to make them a real family?

The tightening in his chest didn't ease when she raised her glass, then gasped at a particularly vivid firework, her eyes gleaming...

Ares wanted to experience these significant moments long after tonight.

'Aren't you having a drink?' she asked.

He shook his head. 'I've had enough of toasts tonight.'

Her eyebrows shot up. 'Chomping at the bit to get on to the next project already?'

The slight quiver in her voice told him she sensed the undercurrents between them.

'Something like that,' he answered easily, even while his stomach churned.

Because this would be his most important project yet.

She lowered her glass, her eyes shadowing slightly, and she winced.

'What is it?' he rasped.

She grimaced, one hand reaching behind her to massage her back. 'I know it's technically impossible, but I feel as if our child has gained another pound between dinner and now!' Her eyes widened as he relieved her of the glass, shed his tuxedo jacket, then dropped to his haunches before her. 'What are you doing?'

He lightly grasped her ankle and unbuckled her shoe. 'Relieving some of your stress—as is my right,' he said, and the pounding need for things he'd thought impossible but which now seemed imperative echoed in his voice.

Her lips parted, but she didn't protest at his assistance, instead bracing one hand on the glass wall and the other on his shoulder. 'Thank you.'

He undid the other shoe and set it aside, then his hands trailed up her slim calves, massaging the firm flesh. His body roared at her husky moan.

'I want to do more,' he offered.

And he meant so much more than easing her aches. Now that he'd given himself fuller permission to envisage their future, endless scenarios bombarded him. One in which the heartache of loss and rejection was frantically overcome with greater, deeper emotion.

*Like love.*

That soul-shaking feeling that had always clung to the edges of his existence and never gone away. No matter how much he'd willed it to. No matter how much he'd convinced himself that this woman wasn't worth it, that her actions were too reminiscent of his pain to ever be set aside.

But now shame stung him for condemning her so roundly. For tainting her and what they might have with the brush of his mother's heartless actions.

She sucked in a shaky breath, then nodded. 'Okay.'

Dropping forward onto his knees, Ares continued his

ministrations, digging into her tight muscles, and watched her head fall back.

'Oh, God, that feels so good.'

Her whispered words sent a powerful sensation straight to his chest, then lower to his lately forsaken libido. He let in the sublime sensation, opening himself up to what could be.

Before he could drive himself insane with the promises whispering in his head he drew out his phone. Keeping one hand on her, and absorbing her every reaction, he sent the electronic command he needed to.

A few minutes later a familiar voice flowed through the inbuilt speakers: *'Ares, your bath is ready.'*

His wife's gaze snapped to his, her beautiful eyes wide in surprise. 'Oh…is that my voice?'

He slotted the phone back into his pocket. 'Yes. I programmed the penthouse virtual assistant to have your voice.' He rose and swept her into his arms.

Her eyes widened even more as her arms slid around his neck. 'It's not in the whole tower, is it?'

Ares shook his head as he strode into the breathtakingly luxurious bathroom. 'No. It's for just this penthouse. For my ears only.'

She shifted in his arms and heat intensified in his groin when another flush crept into her face.

'That pleases you, doesn't it?'

Her beautiful lashes swept down, but he noticed her altered breathing. 'There's something…hot about it,' she murmured sultrily.

'Indeed,' he concurred, stopping next to a tub wide enough to hold six easily.

The lights had been set to a seductive ambience, emphasising her perfection as he reached behind her and lowered her zipper. She was braless, and once he'd disposed of her panties she stood before him, a ripe goddess whom he fully accepted had commanded his world since the first moment she'd stepped into it all those years ago.

'*Thee mou*, you're perfection. Aphrodite herself,' he breathed.

*Mine.* He remembered uttering that possessive on their first night together. That had been a claim from a position of dominance. Now it was more of a plea. A resurgent hope. And it was one he was determined to make a reality, because he was man enough to accept that everything he was, everything he'd achieved, was empty without her.

He glanced at the gently swirling scented water, felt sensation roaring in his ears. 'Alone? Or together?' he asked gruffly.

Breathtaking silver eyes examined him, long and deep. Then she whispered, 'Together.'

The word was barely out of her mouth before he was shucking off his clothes.

He helped her into the tub and washed her body while raining kisses on every inch of exposed skin he could reach. He revelled in her sighs.

Then it was his turn to gasp in wonder as his roved his hands over her swollen belly and felt their child move within.

'He loves that…' She sighed, a captivating smile curving her sensual lips.

'So he should. He's warm and happy.'

Her breath caught, and then she was tilting towards him.

Her eyes searched his again, shades of wariness making him stiffen a little. But before he could petition for himself, step on the road to making things right, she cupped his jaw. Inhaled shakily.

'Ares. Take a chance on this. Take a chance on *us*,' she whispered fervently against his lips.

And, sweet heaven, the way his heart leapt should have terrified every last cell in his body. But it was immediately channelled into a far more satisfying outcome. One he'd been starved of for too long.

A new beginning would work for them.

*It had to.*

He stepped out of the tub and scooped his wife out, his mouth greedily seeking hers as he marched with urgent feet to the bed.

'Ares! I'm wet,' she protested huskily, beautifully, when he set her down next to the emperor-sized bed in the bedroom she'd designed so spectacularly with silver to match her eyes.

His lips curled in a smile he knew reeked of a very masculine satisfaction. 'Yes. And you're about to get wetter, *eros mou.*'

Her deep flush was beautifully predictable. Infinitely arousing.

Ares wanted a lifetime of that.

Tomorrow, he vowed silently to himself, as soon as he was done with slaking this savage hunger, he would embark on making it so.

'Please… Stop torturing me,' she moaned, after he'd spent an age exploring her.

He raised his head from her heated skin, drunk on her beauty. 'But I like watching you come undone for me.'

'Even if the wait torments you too?'

She reached for him, grasped him boldly, and stroked him with enough pressure to siphon the air from his lungs.

'You're a witch.'

'A little while ago I was a goddess,' she tossed back, her half-moon eyes glinting with feminine power.

'Hmm…both are equally enthralling.'

It was the last thing either of them said for a very long time.

'Wake up, sleepyhead.'

Odessa struggled to prise her eyes open. She moaned in

soporific pleasure as firm, warm fingers threaded through her hair and gently massaged her scalp.

'Oh, that feels so good…'

'I'd love to keep going but we've landed. We need to leave the plane.' A soft kiss brushed her temple. 'I'll deliver a full-body massage when we get home if you shift your delicious behind right now,' Ares said, deep amusement in his tone.

'Promise?'

*'Ne.'*

Opening her eyes, she focused on him. His hair was sexily dishevelled, his eyes sharp as he watched her. 'How long did I sleep?'

'Last night or this morning?' he rasped, with a touch of teasing.

She rolled her eyes. 'It's not my fault you wore me out.'

Odessa tensed slightly when his lids swept down, and she felt the edginess she'd had since that telling plea in the bathroom last night return to shimmer over her skin.

She'd sensed something was brewing with Ares. But she'd fallen into an exhausted stupor soon after they'd made love last night and she'd slept in this morning, her heavily pregnant body demanding rest. She'd struggled to dress herself in time to make their plane, and made a beeline for the jet's bedroom as quickly as her waddle could carry her.

Now, after a little rest, she knew she couldn't put this off any longer. 'Can we talk when we get home?'

His amusement evaporated, to be replaced by narrow-eyed intensity. Then he nodded. 'Yes. There are a few things we need to settle, I believe.'

Her nerves intensified, but since she'd initiated this Odessa took a breath and powered through with a nod.

*'Kalos,'* he breathed, and then, rising, swept her into his arms.

Surprised by the move, she linked her arms around his neck. 'I thought I was meant to be walking?'

He shrugged his powerful shoulders and sent her a devilish wink as he exited the bedroom. 'This way gets us moving more quickly.'

She couldn't disagree, so she clung on, hiding her face in his neck when she saw the pilot and flight attendants patiently waiting for them to disembark. She would probably never get used to this level of influential luxury. But she prayed that if it meant being given a chance to remain at Ares's side for the next several decades then she'd learn to live with it.

She was repeating that prayer when they swept into the driveway of his...*their* Athens home.

The promise of a massage—hopefully after she'd pleaded her case once and for all—was very much at the forefront of her mind as Ares sauntered into the large marble foyer of the mansion.

She was preparing appropriate words to express how much she wanted to stay married without the shackles of their agreement when she saw Sergios and a vaguely familiar-looking man approaching from the living room.

With a panicked gasp she realised she was staring at her lawyer—the man she'd only communicated with so far via video call. 'Mr Georgiou. What are you doing here?'

Ares stiffened. 'You know this man?'

Her heart leapt into her throat, both at the lawyer's presence and at the pain and disappointment etched on Sergios's face.

She knew the instant Ares deciphered his father's expression too. He went stiff, his movements careful but stilted as he set her down. A quick glance showed his intensified wariness.

'What's going on?' he rumbled, his eyes scouring her face.

'I… Can we talk in private, please?' she pleaded.

He slanted a glance at the short man, who was grasping rather quickly that his presence here was a big mistake. 'Tell me who you are and what you want with my wife,' Ares demanded, his voice a thin, deadly blade.

The man cast her a deeply apologetic look, then introduced himself. 'I'm your wife's lawyer. We had an appointment yesterday, and when she didn't turn up for our meeting, I thought I'd…'

He spread his hands expressively, while Odessa's heart plummeted.

She'd completely forgotten about the meeting she'd scheduled weeks ago.

The transformation in Ares was heart-stopping. Perhaps it was because it appeared as if he'd stopped breathing as he rounded on her.

'Since when?' he seethed.

Odessa swallowed, her hand darting to her belly as her son chose that moment to kick her—hard. Wincing, she answered, 'A while.'

'How long is "a while"?' Ares demanded.

She cast her mind back, her senses reeling. 'A few weeks.'

Sergios's expression grew harder and Ares sucked in a sharp breath. 'Leave my house. Now.'

The bespectacled man mumbled a quick apology before he darted out through the front door. A purse-lipped Demeter was waiting to shut the door firmly behind him.

Ares's eyes blazed with a mixture of censure and…was it pain?

'That talk you wanted. I'm guessing it has something do with this?'

She shook her head vehemently. 'No! Not this. Ares—'

He stopped her with a raised hand. Glancing around them, he issued a swift order to his father and the staff. With another speaking glance that had her lowering her eyes, Sergios walked away, the staff scurrying after him.

# CHAPTER ELEVEN

ARES STARED AT HER, and a bitter silence throbbed between them.

Then, without speaking, he strode towards his study.

Odessa followed at a slower pace, her mind reeling at how two minutes could completely change the landscape of her life. But while she had a few things to explain, she wasn't giving up.

A sense of *déjà vu* swept over when she entered, to find Ares pacing in front of the mantelpiece.

'You consulted a lawyer?' he rasped, his voice ice-cold shards, his eyes holding the same disbelief, formidable censure and, perhaps most shocking of all, the same pain she'd seen in his father's eyes. 'I want to ask how you could, but what I really should be asking myself is why I believed you'd be different.'

Righteous anger stiffened her spine. 'Don't you dare play that old nonsense with me. You know deep down that you can trust—'

He waved an imperious hand at the door. 'You just proved conclusively that I was a fool to entertain that notion. "Have faith"?' he scoffed, but the edge of his voice was off, something resembling anguish underscoring his words.

'So I made an appointment with a lawyer to talk through my options? So what? Don't you dare judge me for it when you would've done the same in my shoes.' She stopped, shook her head, because the most important thing between them remained unsaid. 'I promise you I was going to cancel. I'd changed my mind about how I needed to tackle this.'

'When?' he threw at her, his frame still frozen in brutal fury. He shook his head before she could speak. 'Don't bother answering that. You only claim you'd changed your mind because you've been caught,' he snarled.

His wan pallor remained, but she didn't believe he was in any way diminished. Hell, she would bet good money that he was feeling immensely, powerfully vindicated right now.

Purpose such as she'd never seen before bristled from him…from the clenched fists to the taut muscles that bunched when he moved. Ares didn't intend to give an inch.

Despair weighed her down as she shook her head. 'Just when I think we're getting somewhere you shatter my hopes.'

His head reared up, vicious emotions bristling from him. 'You have a nerve, speaking of hopes!'

'Do I? Even though I kept repeatedly hanging on to mine even when you pushed me into a corner? What hope did I have when you kept telling me I wasn't good enough to stay in my child's life? But I fought that. You expected me to sit back and take whatever you dish out? How is that rational?'

His jaw clenched. 'If you were so determined to prove me wrong and stay in this marriage, why did you need to seek out a lawyer?'

She sighed in disbelief. 'You see how that works, Ares? You demand unfailing loyalty. But what right do you have to mine when you wouldn't budge about taking away something so vitally important to me?'

'Even if I wouldn't, you've proved that I was once again blind to trust you.'

Odessa was glad she felt numb, because it meant she

didn't crumble over the fact that her heart had shrivelled to nothing. That she was witnessing the end of her marriage— a marriage that had started on extremely shaky ground and only grown shakier.

There would be a time to mourn it—perhaps far too soon and much more devastatingly than she'd feared. Because even in a half-baked marriage she had been the most intensely happy she'd ever been. But for now she raised her chin, refusing to be cowed.

'I won't beg you to believe me. You either do or you don't. But I won't stay here to be vilified for something I haven't done. Feel free to sue me if you wish.'

He laughed, harsh and wicked enough to draw blood. 'And be named a monster just like your father? Or is that what you were counting on? That I would slip up somehow and you could slither your way to the true freedom you want?'

It was her turn to laugh, but she snapped off the sound in under a second before the strong hysteria behind it took hold.

'Look at me, Ares. Do I look like I'm slithering anywhere any time soon?'

When he didn't answer she turned away, viciously swallowing a sob before it could tumble free.

'Where are you going?'

She shrugged. 'I may not have your millions, but I have enough to check in to a hotel for a week or two. Or I'll sleep under a bridge. Who knows? All I know is anywhere you're *not* is good enough for me right now.'

It hurt to say the words. *Badly.* But her heart hurt worse. And she needed a moment or three to lick her wounds.

'Odessa—'

'We have nothing more to say to each other, Ares. Whatever you want to accuse me of next, feel free to tell my lawyer.'

Lies. She would be firing that particular lawyer the first

chance she got. He was just a sweet old man, and he'd proved that the great Ares Zanelis could easily scare him off. She needed someone fearless in her corner for the battle ahead.

'This isn't done,' he said, from far too close behind her.

Her fingers tightened on the door handle. The urge to look back, gorge herself on his image one more time, was overwhelming. By the skin of her teeth, she managed to suppress the temptation.

'Put a hand on me and I'll scream the place down. I called a lawyer before. I'm not above calling the police too.'

She heard his sharp intake of breath and an extremely re-mote part of her almost smiled. She was willing to bet he'd never had a woman say that to him before.

Well, she was also willing to bet he'd never shattered a woman's heart quite as unassailably as he'd demolished hers.

The sense of reprieve she'd wanted withered away when she stepped out of the study, and she only made it halfway down the corridor before true reality struck her. She was walking away from Ares. From her marriage, such as it was. Her heart was ripping itself to pieces and she couldn't breathe.

Her hand shot out, clung to the wall as her legs threatened to give way.

She started when firm hands gripped her arms, but they weren't the hands she craved. Looking up into her father-in-law's eyes was difficult, but she faced him, the knowledge that she'd done nothing wrong burning within her.

'I never… I didn't…' Her voice faltered, tears prickling her eyes.

His lips thinned, but the warmth had returned to his eyes. 'I know.' He looked over his shoulder towards the study. 'I heard some of what happened in there.' He exhaled deeply. 'Putting my son in his place is one thing…opening his eyes

to his faults is another. You'll have to try harder, *mikros*,'
he urged.

Her shattered heart twisted. 'I don't think I can get
through to him.'

His smile was edged in sadness, but the hands holding
hers remained strong. Purposeful. He led her to a chair in
one of the alcoves dotting the corridor, his gaze unwavering as he said, 'You were brought together once more for a
reason. I believe in you.'

Odessa watched him walk away, wishing she could resent him for the burden he'd placed on her.

The burning in her chest remained, unwilling to die. She
turned her face up to the sun beating down through the windows across the hallway. She hated it shining so fiercely
when her whole world had collapsed into darkness.

Nevertheless, she'd closed her eyes and was praying for
strength when the study door opened and slammed, footsteps rushing into the hallway.

Evidently Ares wasn't done with saying his piece either.
For better or worse, they needed to settle this once and for
all.

When the footsteps skidded to a halt, she opened her eyes.
To find a haggard-looking Ares staring at her.

He looked almost...desolate. Frightened. *Pleading.*

'Odessa—'

She held up her hand before she could lose her courage.
'I'm only going to say this once, Ares. Then I'm through.
You don't want my love. I get it. But are you so selfish that
you'd deprive my children too? What will you tell them
when they ask why I'm only around part-time? Because,
yes, I will fight you on full custody. Will you be able to
look them in the eyes and say it's because I don't want to be
with them? Or are you going to admit that you were so terrified to open your heart that you closed theirs to me, too?'

Stark disbelief flashed in his eyes, but hard on its heels came shock, then bewilderment. 'You think I don't want your love?' he rasped, in a bleak, shattered voice.

Her fists bunched in her lap and she cautioned herself to *breathe*.

'Yes. I most certainly do. You've been pushing me away since you turned up at my father's graveside in Alghero. You've used one excuse after another to hold me at arm's length. The moment you could you left Zanzibar, leaving me to chase after you.'

He laughed, a caustic sound that electrified her every nerve-ending.

'You make me sound…' He stopped, took a chest-heaving breath, then shook his head. 'This is far more than just a childish I-pull-your-hair-because-I-like-you playground tactic.'

'You're damn right it is,' she stressed, through teeth gritted so her emotions didn't spill out like a pricked balloon. 'This is my life you're messing with. I know it doesn't mean that much to you, but—'

'No!'

The vehemence of his tone snatched her breath away. Then a red haze wove over her eyes. 'Excuse me? What do you mean, *no*?'

'I mean no, you're not allowed to think for single second that your life doesn't mean that much to me. Not when every damn minute since the moment I set eyes on you you've filled my mind. You've haunted me every single day and night since. I can't make a decision without wondering how you will feel about it. I can't buy a property without wondering whether you would like it, how you would design it if we were together. *Thee mou*… You only need to look at everything I've built and own and you'll find yourself in there somewhere.'

She swallowed, a seismic shift occurring inside her at

the knowledge that she'd guessed right all those weeks ago when she saw the name of the tower.

But that didn't mean... Did it?

'In the months after I left Alghero I could barely function without you.'

Her eyes widened, but the acid in his voice killed her rising elation.

'I'm so sorry that was a hardship for you,' she said.

His hand slashed the air. 'You are a living organism that lives within me. The blood that runs in my veins. I can't take a breath without you. And you... You think I don't love you?'

'*Stronzo!* I'm not a damn psychic! I can't read your mind. And your words and actions have left a lot to be desired.'

His eyes widened. 'Did you just call me an A-hole?'

She stumbled to her feet, glared at him when he jerked towards her, his hands shooting out. 'Yes! Because you deserve it. How was I to know you loved me when you threatened to take away one of the very things we dreamed about? Growing a family together?'

Anguish and shame creased his face. 'It was a knee-jerk reaction to the blows I've been dealt before. I thought I needed to safeguard my heart that already belonged to you. When you rejected our agreement so vehemently I welcomed it, because it meant that you'd stay and fight long after the children were born. That I would have you around one way or another.'

'Let me get this straight... You were willing to tear my heart out of my chest just to test my loyalty and devotion and to keep me around?'

He stared at her with stark intensity for several seconds, then turned and strode towards his study.

Curious despite herself, she followed, to find him at his

desk, rummaging through the papers before he turned with a document in his hand. Striding back, he thrust it at her.

She took it, but didn't remove her gaze from his face. 'Tell me what it says,' she ordered, and the fight in her tone made his eyes widen. 'Now,' she insisted—then gasped when her baby kicked, as if demanding to be heard too.

Ares's eyes grew wider, his hands shooting out reflexively. 'Odessa…?'

'It's just the baby kicking. He's not happy right now, and I don't blame him. I'm far from happy with you myself.'

He swallowed, a wave of jagged emotion that closely resembled panic sweeping over his face. 'That document changes the terms of our agreement.'

'Changes it how?' she demanded.

'There's no time limit on our marriage. You can either leave now…or never. If that's what you…'

He stopped and sucked in a long, shaky breath, and had it been any other time Odessa might have been stunned by this visible show of vulnerability.

But right now she wanted to get to the bottom of their discussion. Because her heart was straining at the bonds tying it down, and the power of that straining was fired up by hope.

Hope she wasn't going to let take over.

*Not yet.*

Perhaps never.

'And there's no petition for full custody,' he went on. 'If you decide to leave after our child is born there'll be no constraints on your participation in his life.'

She swallowed the lump that had been forming at his words. 'You said child—not children. You're willing to let me walk away after he's born? What if I decide to take him with me?'

She noticed the way his eyes shone whenever she referred

to their child, the pulse of love that gleamed for a single moment. But she didn't let that sway her.

*Not yet.*

'*Ne,*' he confirmed. 'Whatever you want. As long as you don't stop me from playing a part in his life.' His face tightened with pain. 'I couldn't bear that.'

Neither could she. Her fingers shook as she grasped the document tighter. 'So what you're saying is that you've changed your mind about everything you wanted without bothering to consult me?'

'Odessa—'

'What makes you think I want just one child? You know that I hated growing up alone! That, like you, I wanted to find healing in a big family who love and care for each other. That I want to be the kind of mother we both wanted for our children.'

The hand he speared through his hair visibly shook. 'I was too afraid to hope for it, Odessa. What my father and I went through…' He stopped, and swallowed, then exhaled heavily. 'I wouldn't wish it on my worst enemy. And even the smallest possibility that it could happen again was unthinkable to me. It was easier to build my life around the fact that it would one day manifest in some shape or form and take steps to guard myself against it.'

She tossed the paper away, pain ripping her apart. 'You know what I went through with my own father. What he did to my mother. How could you think that I would ever do something like that to my own child?'

A flash of shame darted over his face. 'I didn't. Not for the most part. But…cruelty isn't the only weapon. When I fell deeper in love with you I felt a different sort of terror. How could you love me back when I had put my own goals in front of your desires?' he said in a barely audible rasp.

He squeezed his eyes shut, both hands gripping his nape

in a move of despair so unlike him her shattered heart bled—not for herself this time, but for him.

'I've ruined everything, haven't I?' he asked bleakly.

Her eyes fell to the paper on the floor, then she grasped his hands as he lowered them. 'All you had to do was let me in, Ares. Talk me through what you were feeling. Then I would have told you that I've never stopped loving you. Not when I was sixteen and too shy to talk to the boy with the golden hazel eyes. Nor when I turned seventeen and lay with you beneath the stars, knowing it was the happiest time of my life so far. Not even when you left without saying goodbye and I cried myself to sleep for months. And I love you now because you have fulfilled one of my many dreams by becoming the father of the child I always hoped to have. All that is left now is for you to fulfil my greatest wish. Be the love of my life that I've prayed you'd be from the moment I saw you.'

His jaw had been gaping since she'd started speaking. Now he stared, wide-eyed, as if she was the most entrancing thing he'd ever seen, his fingers tightening around hers.

'*Thee mou*, Odessa…'

'Don't keep me waiting, Ares,' she implored desperately. 'Make my dreams come true. Please.'

He took a single lunge towards her and swept her into his arms, a shudder moving through him as he folded her close. 'Yes. I don't deserve you, but… Please… *Yes*. To every single one of them. My remaining years will be devoted to you and our child…our children. I love you so much, Odessa. I'm so sorry I let the past get in the way of our future.'

She pulled back far enough to cradle his jaw. 'And I'm so sorry about what happened to your sister.'

His eyes glittered with emotion and he swallowed before he nodded. 'I've tortured myself with whether I could've done more…'

'You were a child yourself. And Sergios needs to forgive himself for not reading the signs earlier. It's time for you both to live the life she would've wanted you to. Remember her with love, not with pain, and honour her by being happy.'

He pressed his forehead to hers. 'I almost let my fears get in the way. For that I'm sorry, *eros mou*.'

She indicated the piece of paper. 'You were prepared to sacrifice your own wishes for me. It means the world to me, but I'm so glad we don't have to be apart, Ares.'

Another shudder moved through him. 'Never. For as long as I have breath in my body we will be together. *Always*.'

His firm, gruff vow was sealed with a deep kiss that swept away the last of her fears and misgivings, leaving only hope and ocean-deep love.

They were still kissing, still whispering fervent words of love, when a throat was cleared.

Sergios stood on the threshold, a mile-wide smile on his face. 'Pardon the intrusion, but spare an old man's heart and tell me this little turbulence is behind us?'

Their unborn son kicked hard, happy and content and strong enough for Ares to feel it. His face was transformed in absolute awe and, laughing at his expression, she answered Sergios.

'It's smooth sailing ahead, Baba.'

His eyes filled at the affectionate term, and he approached, arms outstretched. After a warm, loving hug, he slapped his still-silent son on the back, nodded once, then left them alone.

Ares, his hand still on her belly, dropped another kiss to her lips. 'I love you, *kardia mou*. So very much.'

'*S'agapo*,' she echoed, her heart full to overflowing.

# EPILOGUE

*Three years later*

'YOU HAVE YOUR two babies, Kyrios Zanelis. Now what?' Odessa teased him from her private hospital bed.

Yellow roses, her favourite flowers, covered every spare surface in the room and on her bedside, a large picture of them with Paris, their almost three-year-old son, continually drew his eye, even though the flesh and blood versions were right there in the room with him.

Ares stared at his wife, glowing and exhausted from bringing their second child into the world only four hours ago.

How she still managed to be the most beautiful woman in the world was beyond him. Perhaps one day, decades from now, he would stop wondering how he'd got so lucky.

For now…he stared down at his new daughter, the pull and twinge in his chest building until he couldn't quite catch his breath.

'Two more, at the very least,' he answered. Then, based on pure greed, he added, 'Or three if we can manage it. Please.'

She laughed, flinging back the hair he'd lovingly brushed ten minutes ago, making his heart flip over several risky times. 'You drive a hard bargain, *agapo*.'

Her husky endearment, one of many he'd been privileged to receive from her in the last three years, made his heart somersault a few more times. He never tired of the feelings. And dear God, he hoped he never did.

'It's hard not to when you show me every day what it's like to be surrounded by so much love. So much happiness. You know I'm a greedy man, *agapita*. This sleeping beauty in my arms and the little rascal making his grandfather laugh hard enough to bring tears to his eyes, makes me want as many such treasures as you can gift me.'

'She's beautiful, isn't she? They both are,' she said with a happy sigh, her gaze lingering on him in a way that made his whole being light up with impossible joy.

Emotion clogged his throat as he looked down at his daughter, the child they'd already decided to name after his late sister, Sofia.

'They have your beautiful eyes,' he murmured, the wonder of it overwhelming him anew. 'I prayed they would, and now I'm two for two.' *Ne*, there was a hint of smugness in his tone, but he could live with it.

'You prayed?' There was teasing. But there was also devotion. Promises given and offered back.

He looked up, met those silver eyes that had stolen his heart the first moment, even though he'd fought it far too long. 'Oh, yes. From the moment I saw you, I wanted babies with you. Babies with eyes exactly like yours.'

'Ares,' she breathed his name and like a magnet compelling him to her side, he approached her bed.

With his free hand, he meshed his fingers with hers, drew them to his lips and dropped kisses on them. 'I love you. *Efkharisto.*'

'*Efkharisto,*' his father echoed, looking up from kissing his grandson's chubby cheeks with a tell-tale sheen in his eyes.

Ares shook his head and glanced over at his father. 'No, Baba. It is I who should thank you, for making me see that my future was with Odessa and making me take you back to Alghero.'

Sergios nodded. 'We all won in the end, *yios*.'

'Yes, we did,' his beautiful, sleepy wife murmured from within his arms, her fingers finding and lovingly cradling his cheek as she smiled up at him. 'Love brought us home.'

\* \* \* \* \*

*Were you blown away by*
Greek Pregnancy Clause?
*Then don't miss out on these*
*other dramatic stories*
*by Maya Blake!*

His Pregnant Desert Queen
The Greek's Forgotten Marriage
Pregnant and Stolen by the Tycoon
Snowbound with the Irresistible Sicilian
Accidentally Wearing the Argentinian's Ring

*Available now!*